DADDY

KINKY BOYS BOOK 1

NORA PHOENIX
K.M. NEUHOLD

Daddy (Kinky Boys book one) by K.M. Neuhold and Nora Phoenix

Copyright ©2020 K.M. Neuhold and Nora Phoenix

Cover design: Vicki Brostenianc www.vickibrostenianc.com

Editing: Tanja Ongkiehong

All rights reserved. No part of this story may be used, reproduced, or transmitted in any form by any means without the written permission of the copyright holder, except in case of brief quotations and embodied within critical reviews and articles.

This is a work of fiction. Names, characters, places, and incidents either are the products of the author's imagination or are used fictitiously. Any resemblance to actual persons, living or dead, businesses, companies, events, or locales is entirely coincidental. The use of any real company and/or product names is for literary effect only. All other trademarks and copyrights are the property of their respective owners.

This book contains sexually explicit material which is suitable only for mature readers.

1

JOEY

The sounds of grunts and moans and slapping skin echo from farther away as I make my way down the hallway to Bear's office. Since we've already wrapped filming for the day, I guess Tank and Brewer decided to enjoy an off-camera round two rather than hitting the showers straight away.

A pang of regret hits me in the chest. I've looked at this problem a million ways, and unfortunately, the only right choice is the one I really wish I didn't have to make.

I've been the head cameraman for the Ballsy Boys porn studio for the better part of a decade. Filming gay porn might seem like an odd career path for a straight man, but it's never bothered me. Don't get me wrong. This wasn't the career I envisioned when I went to film school. But I certainly can't complain. I fell into it when I needed money, and I found a sense of pride in it. The vast majority of the public might look down on the porn industry, but I've seen firsthand just how hard these guys work—no pun intended —and I love knowing that I have a hand in the quality of the final product we put out.

Bear took a chance on me when this studio was a fledgling, and I've come to see him as a friend. Which makes the decision I have to make that much more difficult.

I slow my steps as I draw close to Bear's office, trying to think of any excuse to put off the inevitable. But that's just the problem. I've been putting this off for weeks at this point, and it's time to rip off the Band-Aid.

I rap my knuckles against the sturdy oak door and hold my breath.

"Come in," Bear calls out.

I turn the knob and push it open slowly, the door creaking ominously as I do. I've learned to always open Bear's door slowly to give anyone—namely his boyfriend, Pixie—time to put their pants back on if needed. Not that Pixie minds being caught naked. Hell, he was one of the stars here until he started dating Bear, so I've seen him a lot more than just naked. These days his nudity is just for Bear...and anyone who happens to open the door to Bear's office too abruptly.

Peeking my head inside, I find both Bear and Pixie fully dressed, at least from what I can see. Pixie's seated on Bear's lap behind the large desk. He has a serious expression on his face that only lasts for a few seconds before it turns into a grin.

"Hey, Joey," Pixie greets enthusiastically.

"Hey, I hope I'm not interrupting anything?" I glance between the two men, my eyes lingering on Bear's arm, which is secured possessively around Pixie's waist as he leans back into the large man, looking as comfortable and safe as can be. A strange tingle runs down my spine, and my throat feels a little too tight for just a few seconds.

"A little," Pixie says, and Bear makes a small rumbly noise.

"Behave," he scolds gently, and Pixie giggles.

"Sorry, Daddy."

My chest constricts, and I consider backing out of the room and saving this conversation for another day. Except I don't have another day. The movers are set to show up at my place on Saturday, which means I'm already the asshole who isn't giving two weeks' notice because I spent so long trying to work up the nerve to quit.

"What's up?" Bear asks, training his attention on me.

"I'm not sure how to do this," I admit, running a hand through my hair.

"You're quitting?" he guesses, and I nod. The air whooshes out of my lungs with relief that he picked up on it so quickly. He's good like that. He always seems to have a weird, innate perceptiveness of people I never quite understood. I'm sure that's part of what makes him such a good… Daddy, as Pixie calls him.

After I first heard Pixie refer to him that way, I tested the word out on my tongue a few times at home. Not that I'd never heard it before, but it was different, knowing it existed versus the reverent way Pixie whispered it when they filmed a scene together not long ago.

I don't know why it stuck with me after the shoot, why I couldn't shake it for weeks afterward. I wondered at first if some part of me wanted a beautiful woman in my lap the way Pixie is in Bear's, calling me Daddy and looking at me with wide, wanting eyes. But that didn't fit.

Maybe it's that I haven't met the right woman. That has to be the answer to why nothing has ever felt exactly right. Why I never have trouble appreciating beauty but never seem to respond the way others do by immediately wanting to whisk someone attractive away to my bed.

Bear looks at me with patient expectation, and I realize I should probably tell him why I need to leave.

I clear my throat. "I don't want to go, and I'm sorry I have to give you such short notice, but it's my mom," I explain. "She's not doing well. We had to move her into a care facility after her last incident when she wandered off and forgot where the house was. So now my dad's living all alone, and I don't know how much longer my mom has before she won't recognize me at all, but I need to go."

"Of course you need to go," Bear agrees. "Didn't you say your parents live in Las Vegas?"

"Yeah, why?"

"Well, if you're interested, Hunter is still working on getting things fully off the ground for the Kinky Boys studio. I'm sure he'd love to have you on board."

"Don't you mean *Daddy*," Pixie teases, and Bear raises an eyebrow at him.

"You know who your Daddy is, baby boy, and it sure as hell isn't Hunter."

"No, it's not," Pixie agrees, giving Bear a loud kiss on the cheek.

"I'll give him a call to let him know you'll be moving to town and shoot him your number if you'd like," he offers.

"That would be great," I say with relief. The thought of looking for a new job was one I was dreading almost as much as actually having to quit.

"If there's anything else I can do to help you out, you'll let me know." It's not a question, and I don't have any choice but to nod.

"I appreciate it. Everything you've done means so much to me. I really owe you," I say.

"Pay it forward. You helped me build this studio, and

now you can help my best friend do the same. I'm sure he can use the hand."

An image of the confident, sure man who walked in here six months ago and told Bear he was opening his own porn studio flashes through my mind, and I snort a laugh, imagining him needing help with anything, let alone needing it from me. But if Bear thinks I'm the man for the job, I'll do my damnedest to do him proud.

Daddy

Las Vegas in the early morning is nothing like Las Vegas at night. It's like waking up in a strange bed after a one-night stand and wondering what the hell you were thinking going home with *that*. At night, this city is blinding, fun, attractive, and exciting. Kinda like that guy looked when you were drunk off your ass. In the morning, all that's left is a sun that's too bright, a blue sky that seems to mock you as you step out, and a massive hangover.

Aren't I delightful in the morning? Look, I'm from New York. I'm predisposed to hate everything on sight, even though the reality is that Sin City—and there's a name locals would never use—has treated me far better than New York did. But let's not go there, because that topic will ruin my mood for sure. And as we already concluded, I'm not exactly Mr. Sunshine in the early morning.

Thank fuck the nearest Starbucks is only two blocks from my house. After drinking half of my Venti Americano with a Shot in the Dark and one pump vanilla—it took me a year of fine-tuning to get my coffee exactly the way I like it—

I feel better. At least, my head is clearer, and that's important because I have a job interview first thing on the schedule this morning. Not for a job for me but for the porn studio I'm trying to get started here. Emphasis on *trying*.

My old friend, Bear, owner of the renowned and highly rated Ballsy Boys studio, called me a few days ago, telling me that his best cameraman, Joey, was moving to Vegas and would I be interested in hiring him? I don't think I've ever said yes to anything faster in my life, including propositions of some of the sexiest, sweetest boys who offered themselves to me.

So here we are, and I'll be interviewing Joey. The truth is that this interview is a farce. Obviously, I'm not telling Joey that. If I want to appear like a reputable business, I have to go through the motions of pretending he's one of many candidates. In reality, he's it.

Look, I did get a whole inbox full of reactions to my job ad for a cameraman. It's gay porn, for fuck's sake. It's not like I'd have trouble finding someone who wants to film it. The challenge is finding someone who has more experience than shooting a home porn on his iPhone.

Joey checks all the boxes, with a glowing recommendation from Bear as a nice red bow wrapped around it. He's won *awards* for his camera work. No way in hell am I saying no to *that* package. But I'll be damned if I show him my hand and come across as desperate as I am. If Bear hadn't called me, I don't know what I would've done.

Joey is not what I'd expected when I first spot him sitting in the shared waiting room of the complex where I'm renting a small office. He's looking at his phone, which gives me the opportunity to study him. He's about my age, I estimate, maybe a few years younger, but it can't be much. His build is much more slender than mine, like it usually is with men. Let's just say I spend a lot of time in the gym to work through my *issues*. Unlike mine, his hair only has silver sprinkled in at his temples but is dark and messy elsewhere.

I like his look. In the business I'm in, you meet a lot of fake people, over-the-top folks who need attention like it's a drug. It probably is to them. But Joey looks wonderfully wholesome in his jeans and button-up shirt, which he probably only threw on to at least make an effort to wear something respectable to this interview. I can tell by the way his finger pulls back the collar every now and then. He's cute—though that is a bit of a weird expression for a man my age, I guess.

"Joey?" I ask, stepping farther into the waiting room.

He looks up, immediately closing his phone. "Yes. I take it you're Mr. Tronco?"

I nod as we shake hands. "Call me Hunter. Like Bear, I run a relaxed operation here."

Joey glances around the waiting room. "I was under the impression you were running a studio, but this doesn't seem to be the right place for that."

He's smart, perceptive. "It's not. I'm putting the final touches on a building I've leased to make it suitable for our purposes. This is just a temporary office so I don't have to work from my rather cramped two-bedroom apartment."

"Gotcha."

He follows me into the office, and I gesture for him to take a seat across from me. "Did Bear tell you anything about what I'm starting here?"

Joey nods. "Kinky Boys, right? It's like the kink version of the Ballsy Boys, if I understand correctly."

I take a few minutes to share my vision for the studio

with him: high-quality videos that show how beautiful kink can be but that also demonstrate how to do it safely and consensually. It's a project I'm deeply passionate about, as it combines my love for and experience with kink and my appreciation for high-quality gay porn.

Joey listens attentively, then asks a few questions about the technical side of business, showing he's a far more qualified cameraman than I could have ever dreamed to recruit. If I hadn't already decided to hire him before he even showed up, this would've done the job. He's gonna kill it.

"I have one guy who's just getting his feet wet as a cameraman," I say. "He has some experience shooting a wide variety of YouTube-style videos, but this is his first foray into porn. His name is Silas. One of your responsibilities would also be to train him and mentor him."

"Sure," Joey says. "No problem."

Since I already asked Bear how much he made working for him, I offer him the same salary, which should be, in reality, an increase as the cost of living here is slightly lower than in LA. Joey agrees, and that leaves me with one more question, an uncomfortable one but one I feel like I have to ask.

"Forgive me for asking because believe me, I'm well aware of how extremely personal this is and probably also ten kinds of illegal, but do you have a boyfriend? I want to avoid any trouble with the boys who will be working for me. It may sound strange, but I'm quite protective of them, and I want to make sure this working environment is safe for them. If you're in a committed relationship, that would be a huge plus. Not that people never cheat, but at least you may not be as tempted."

Joey shifts in his seat, and for the first time in the interview, he seems uncomfortable. "I'm not gay," he finally says after squirming a bit more. "I'm straight."

"You're what now?" I blink a few times, certain I must have misheard him.

"I'm straight," he repeats, his voice a little louder now.

"You're straight."

"Yeah."

"You've worked in gay porn for over ten years, but you're straight?"

Joey squares his shoulders. "Look, I'm damn good at what I do, okay? It shouldn't make a difference who I fuck. Or love."

In theory, he's right of course, but the reality is that I have questions. Quite a few, actually. "How the hell can you work in gay porn if you're straight?" I ask the most obvious one.

Joey shrugs. "It's a job. Bear is a great boss, who has always given me a lot of creative freedom, the boys have been amazing and nice to me, and it's a fun, relaxed atmosphere to work in. What's not to love? And it's not like I have anything against gay porn. To each his own and all that. I'd say it makes me even better at my job because I can focus on getting the best shot possible without getting distracted by what's happening in front of me. And most of all: I'm the cameraman. I film. I don't, you know, fuck anyone myself, so at the end of the day, it doesn't matter who or what I'm attracted to."

I ponder this for a bit, imagining myself working in straight porn. I love women, don't get me wrong, and some of my best friends are women, but I'm not attracted to them in the least. I'm not sure I could watch them have sex day in, day out. For ten fucking years.

But I have to admit that, looking at Joey again, I don't get a gay vibe from him at all. Nothing. He's not even straight-passing; he's...straight. *Huh.* Looks like he's telling the truth. Well, that solves one problem because if he's not gay, at least I won't have to worry about him getting inappropriate with one of the boys.

I extend my hand to him. "Welcome to Kinky Boys, Joey. I'm excited to have you on board."

2

JOEY

"One last question," I ask, my hand on the doorknob, turning back to Hunter. "What's your timeline looking like? You said the space is still being renovated. Is everything else set to go?"

A chagrined look passes over the man's face before he masks it with another calm, confident grin.

"Not exactly," he admits. "I have a lot of submission tapes, of course, but very few of them *feel* right."

"So, we don't have a space to film yet, and we don't have any models *to* film. What exactly do we have?"

"The best cameraman in the business if Bear is to be believed," he answers smoothly, and something about the praise, even if it's more indirect praise from Bear than anything, warms the pit of my stomach. "I was certainly impressed watching you work your camera magic when you filmed the scene with Bear and Pixie to debut Kinky Boys."

I give a quick nod. "Thanks. If there's anything I can help you with, give me a call anytime."

"Thank you."

As soon as I leave the meeting with Hunter, I unbutton

my shirt, freeing myself from the irritating pull of the too-tight collar around my neck, and toss it onto the passenger seat of my car. I shrug my shoulders to get my plain white undershirt to sit right and then roll my neck to work out the stress kinks that worked their way in while I was waiting for my interview to start. I figured I was a shoo-in, but I didn't want to assume anything. Besides, it's always better to start off on a professional note in these sorts of situations.

I'm not sure why I offered him my help like that anyway. Sure, I worked with Bear, but it's not like I know a hell of a lot about setting up a studio. I do my magic behind the camera. Beyond that, I can't say I have many talents. I'm no good at relationships of any kind. I couldn't even be the kind of filmmaker my parents wanted me to be. They were totally on board with film school when they thought I was going to be the next Steven Spielberg, but once they found out I was filming porn, well...they weren't thrilled.

I have *one* thing going for me, and that's my camera lens.

I start my car and sigh happily as the icy air conditioning blasts out of the vents, cooling the droplets of sweat already forming on my skin after the short walk from the office building to my car.

I run my hands through my hair and put the address of the care facility into my phone. I spent my first week here getting my new apartment set up and anxiously awaiting my meeting with Hunter. With that out of the way and my place cleared of any moving boxes, I can't think of another excuse to avoid visiting her.

As soon as I pull into the parking lot of the facility, it's obvious that at least half of the exorbitant amount of money I'm spending on this place every month is going to aesthetics. If the enormous fountain out front and the immaculate garden are supposed to somehow help me feel better about the fact that my mom only knows who I am on good days, they're not working.

Tilting my head back against my headrest, I take a deep breath, working up the nerve to go in there. When my aunt called me last month and told me my mom was picked up by the police, wandering the streets in the middle of the night for the third time in as many weeks, it felt like a boulder was sitting in my stomach.

I never minded being an only child, but I suddenly wished like hell that I had a brother or sister to help shoulder this burden with me. But no siblings meant it had been up to me to break it to my dad that I thought it was best to put Mom somewhere where they could watch her better. And boy did *that* go over well. In the end, it was my aunt who helped convince him.

It takes me about ten minutes sitting in the parking lot before I manage to get out of the car and make my way inside. A receptionist greets me. I wonder if she's the one my aunt keeps going on about in a less than subtle way, telling me all about how pretty and helpful she is and how I would *just love her*. She picked up right where my mother had left off in trying to get me to settle down and start a family already. As if I don't want that too. As if I haven't spent over a decade trying to find the right woman. Maybe a happily ever after just isn't in the cards for me.

"Hi, I'm Julie. How can I help you?" She flashes me a toothy smile full of perfectly straight white teeth. I didn't even know teeth could be that white; they're almost blinding. I resist the urge to shield my eyes against the glare bouncing off her teeth and offer her a smile in return instead.

"Hi, I'm here to visit my mom, Dorothy Finch."

"Oh Dorothy, she is such a sweetheart," Julie gushes, and

I wonder if she says that about all the residents or if the Alzheimer's has somehow made my mom less of a chore.

"Yeah," I agree, keeping my smile in place.

"She should be in the common room right about now. You can head straight down the hall and follow the sound of *Wheel of Fortune*," she says with a chuckle.

"Great, thanks." I look at her for a few more seconds. Aside from the freakishly white teeth, she *is* cute. I wait for something to stir inside me, anything more than the vaguest sense of interest, something like what other people seem to feel when they find someone attractive. Nothing happens, so I offer her one last cordial smile before heading down the hallway.

As promised, I find my mom sitting in a chair in the common room with *Wheel of Fortune* playing on the television. She's staring somewhat blankly, and my stomach drops. Shifting on my feet, I wonder if there's even a point to being here if she won't know who I am today.

She glances in my direction, and I grab an empty chair to pull up beside her.

"Hi, Mom," I greet her gently. She blinks at me, a look of confusion passing behind her eyes.

"Hello, Jerry," she says after a short pause.

The first time she called me by the name of her dead brother three years ago, we both laughed it off. Over the next year, my aunt called me almost weekly, becoming more and more concerned as my mom grew more forgetful and more irritable. It started with small things: forgetting where she parked her car or left her keys, not remembering what she read in the newspaper that morning, mixing up names more frequently. When we finally got the Alzheimer's diagnosis, she was already in the second stage.

The worst part is that sometimes it's almost easier when

she thinks I'm Jerry. I don't have to argue with her about my job or answer questions about why I haven't met a nice girl yet.

"How are you?" I ask.

"Jerry, I have to tell you something," she says sadly, and my stomach twists at the painful expression on her face. She reaches for me and grabs my hand in a strong grip. "I'm the one who hid cigarettes in the garage, and when Mom found them, I said they were yours."

"It's okay," I assure her, patting her hand. "I forgive you."

She sags with relief and smiles. "Do you want to go to Sparky's and get a cheeseburger?"

"Not right now. Why don't we sit here a little while?" I suggest.

"Okay."

For the next two hours, we watch whatever insipid gameshow happens to come on, and then I take my leave, promising her I'll visit again later in the week, even though I don't expect her to remember it.

When I get back to my apartment, I sink onto my couch and kick off my shoes, imagining what it would be like to have a partner to come home to, someone to share the burdens of my day with. Then I chuckle and shake my head at myself because apparently I don't even need my mom or my aunt to make me feel bad about being single. I can handle that job all on my own.

3
JOEY

The last thing I expected at nine o'clock on a Saturday night is a text from Hunter. I stare at the phone for a few seconds before unlocking it to read the message.

Hunter: Were you serious when you offered help?

I BITE MY BOTTOM LIP, considering the question. Of course, I'm more than happy to help him however I can to get Kinky Boys up and running. But what kind of help can *I* offer at this time of night on a Saturday?

Joey: Sure. What do you need?
Hunter: Meet me down on The Strip?
Joey: What? Now?
Hunter: Yeah, and in the next half hour if you can manage it. Sorry for the short notice

I GLANCE down at my laid-back attire—a pair of gray sweats and a comfortable black T-shirt. Dragging my fingers through my hair, I sit up and look around a little helplessly as if some fairy godmother is going to appear and poof me something more acceptable to wear, since I haven't gotten around to doing laundry yet this week.

Joey: Does it have to be tonight?
Hunter: Ideally, but if you can't make it, I understand

I HUFF OUT A BREATH. It's not that I *can't* make it. It's just that I generally prefer at least twenty-four hours to mentally prepare to be social if I can help it. But I *did* promise to give him a hand with setting up the studio.

Joey: I can be there. I'll see you in twenty
Hunter: I knew I liked you

I CONSIDER THROWING on a pair of jeans from my dirty clothes hamper but decide not to bother. Wherever we're going, it's not like I'm all that wound up about looking hot. I've long since passed the stage in my life where I give a shit about impressing anyone. I take a few seconds to brush my teeth and then shove my shoes on, and I'm out the door.

Hunter sends me his exact location, and I manage to make it to him just under the wire. As I approach him, I notice him before he spots me. He's leaning against the side of a building, radiating the kind of confidence I've only ever dreamed of. There's something about the set of his shoulders and the way he carries himself that seems to shout to the world that he's in charge. Bear has the same quality, but it's even more pronounced in Hunter. It's no wonder he goes by Daddy most of the time. I bet he takes good care of the boys in his charge.

Something about that thought sends a little shiver down

my spine that I can't quite place. His gaze is sweeping the busy sidewalk like he's sizing up every person who passes him. Then his attention lands on me, and it feels like it holds me in my spot. His steel-gray eyes are sharp as they rake over me, and a smile twists his lips as amusement seems to crinkle at the corners of his eyes.

"Gray sweatpants and a T-shirt, *that's* what you wear out on the town?"

I shrink in on myself with embarrassment. "You said to hurry, so I didn't bother to change. Sorry, I can run home and put on something that'll look better."

"I didn't say you didn't look good," he says, his voice dipping lower. "It was surprising, but I don't have any objection. Besides, there's no time for you to change. We're going to miss the start of the show if we don't go in."

"Go in to what?" I ask, looking at the building behind us. It seems to be a hotel and casino, nothing out of the ordinary for downtown Vegas.

"Mantasia," he answers with a smirk.

"Hold on. You made me hurry down here so we could watch a bunch of guys dance and show off their abs? And this is helping the business, how exactly?"

"We're looking for talent," he explains, pushing fully off the wall and leading me over to the entrance.

"Talent?" I repeat, feeling like I must've missed some sort of punchline. "Like guys for the studio? Didn't you get a bunch of audition tapes?"

"I did, but so few of them...*inspired* me."

"So, now we're going to watch some guys dance half naked, and you're going to pick your favorites to try to recruit away from *this* job to work for you? That seems unethical."

"I'm going to give them options. That's not unethical."

"I don't understand where I come in. You heard the part about me being straight, right? It's not like I'm going to be able to weigh in on the hottest guy here," I point out.

"Maybe not, but after more than ten years filming for Ballsy Boys, I'm guessing you have quite an eye for talent. You've seen men come and go from that studio. You've seen the career guys and the dabblers, and you've filmed them all. If anyone knows what makes a true star, I'm betting it's you."

The confidence in his voice as he pours on the praise makes me preen a little. I suppose he's not wrong. Over the years, I've learned to spot the guys who are going to last versus the ones who find shame in the profession or simply think it's a bit of fun for a summer before they move on to whatever their next outrageous story will be.

"Okay, yeah, I guess I can help with this," I agree.

"I thought so."

Hunter pats me on the shoulder, and I lean into the feeling for a second. My parents were never much for physical affection, and in the relationships I've had, it always seemed like the women expected the barest touch to lead to the bedroom. I know most men have sex on their minds constantly, but it's never been a top priority for me. I do love touch, though—hugging, cuddling, holding hands. Why can't that be enough for more people? And clearly I've been single too long if a friendly pat on the shoulder has my mind wandering so far down this path.

We head up to the second floor, where Mantasia goes on. Hunter gives our tickets at the entrance for the show, and I follow him inside. For the most part, it's exactly what I expected, a large stage front and center, with a few platforms peppered between the tables. There's a mix of men and women, definitely trending more toward women, and the heavy scent of alcohol hangs in the air.

We claim our seats, and both order a couple of outrageously priced drinks. Onstage, on the background screen, a video is playing of the guys who are in the show doing manly things without shirts on while music plays. I take the opportunity to size up each of them with an objective eye for their build and overall demeanor—who seems the most comfortable and relaxed versus who appears to be putting on more of a show about the whole thing.

By the time it gets underway, I already have a couple of guys in mind for potential candidates. My chest thumps with the bass music that thunders through the theater. The men now onstage dance energetically. I sip my drink and pay attention to the way each of them move, cataloging their grace and enthusiasm so I can form a full opinion.

Hunter seems to be doing the same, but it's obvious he's having a lot more fun than I am. A predatory glint enters his eyes, and a bulge forms in the front of his jeans. Not that I'm *looking* at the front of his jeans. I just happen to notice.

He whistles and cheers as the first routine ends. The men exit the stage, and the backlighting dims as a fully dressed man takes center stage. He seems to be the emcee of the show, welcoming us and giving a little background about the guys while throwing in a few off-color jokes and eliciting some cheers. While he talks, a smaller man scurries onto the stage, places a chair, and picks up pieces of the tear-away pants that are left there from the first routine. It's difficult to see much of him in the darkness of the stage, but something about him reminds me a bit of Pixie. Maybe it's his slight build or the way he moves; I can't quite place my finger on it.

The music starts up again, and the muscular men return

to the stage to do a new dance for us. This time they make more use of the other stages in the audience as well as move into the crowd to grind and flirt. One of the men ends up in Hunter's lap, in nothing more than a thong, and Hunter doesn't seem to mind it one bit. The man does have nice muscles. He'd probably look great on film.

The show feels like it lasts ages. After the first two routines, it's more of the same: dancing, grinding, pulling giggling men and women up onto the stage to simulate sex with them for the cheering audience. If you ask me, it could've been half as long, but what do I know?

When the lights come on, Hunter turns to me, a look of determination coloring his features.

"I have a few ideas for who might be a good fit," I say, standing and following him toward the exit. He's moving fast, his stride purposeful.

"I saw the perfect boy," he says easily. "Come on, let's hurry so we don't miss him."

"You're going to offer one of these guys a job right now while they're getting groped by drunk people after their show? Wouldn't it be better to try to talk to them later?"

He ignores my question, leading me around to the stage entrance. He glances both ways to make sure security isn't right behind us and then slips through the door. I follow him in a hurry, holding my breath and looking over my shoulder. We are *so* going to get busted and thrown out.

"Where are we going? All the guys are in that lounge right across from the theater entrance."

Again, Hunter doesn't respond, coming to a halt in front of me. I look around him to see the stagehand organizing the various chairs into their proper places now that the show is over.

"Him?" I ask, seeing the excited flash in Hunter's eyes.

"Him."

Daddy

God, he's perfect. He's the epitome of a twink, with a slender, graceful body that is stronger than it appears, since he easily lifts those heavy chairs to put everything back in order. I love the way he moves. It's effortlessly, almost like he's floating.

"Hi," I say softly as not to jostle him.

His head snaps back at my voice. He gives me a quick once-over, then does the same with Joey. His eyes radiate distrust, which I can't blame him for. "Can I help you? Pretty sure you're not supposed to be here."

"I hope so," I say, ignoring the last part of his statement, and I hold out my business card. "My name is Hunter Tronco, and I run a movie production company here in Vegas. This here is my head cameraman, Joey."

He chuckles as he takes the card, not even looking at it. "Is this where you tell me I will be the new Leonardo DiCaprio or some BS? Because I've been there, done that, and no T-shirt is worth going through that shit again."

Oh, boy, he's got sass. I love me some sassy boys. It does tell me that being upfront will work best. "Those are not the kind of movies I make."

He narrows his eyes, then looks at the business card in his hand. I can see the exact point when it hits him because his eyes widen before he looks up again. "Porn. That's what you make, right? Porn."

I recognize the disdain in his voice. I've heard it often enough not just in the last few weeks but even before that, when I still owned Balls to the Walls, my club in New York. Owning a gentlemen's club that caters to straight men is one thing, but apparently in the hierarchy of entertainment, owning a gay BSDM club ranks somewhere down the bottom, right about where gay porn is.

So I square my shoulders because I've never been, nor will I ever be ashamed of who I am and what I do. "Not just porn. High-quality, gay, kinky porn."

"And let me guess. To audition, I need to sleep with you."

Wow, cynical much? There's a story there, I'm sure, but now is not the time and the place to get into that. "Actually, no. That would break all kinds of rules, and I'm not only talking about my own moral code but a few laws as well."

He leans back against a stack of chairs, his posture still defensive. "What's your spiel, then?"

"My spiel?"

"Your sales pitch, your elevator pitch, the magical words that you say to everyone before they throw themselves at your feet and beg you to take them."

This is not going how I envisioned it, but fuck if I'm not highly entertained. "To have boys throw themselves at my feet and beg me to take them, I usually only have to show up in my leather pants, bare-chested, and ask which boy wants to find a new religion on my cock, but that's not what I'm going for here."

His mouth pulls up in a hint of a smile. "My experience is that men who promise you heaven have no fucking clue what that place actually looks like."

"I can assure you I've not only seen heaven but also the whole universe and all the stars, and I sure as fuck could take you there if I were so inclined, but that's for another day."

"I'll take your word for it. So tell me what you want from me."

"Have you ever considered going into porn?" I ask directly.

He shrugs. "Sure. Hasn't everyone in this town? At some point, we're all desperate enough, right?"

I shake my head. "I prefer people who do it because they love it. Desperation will only get you so far. The ones who are most successful at it are the ones who do it because they love having sex. They're proud of their bodies, of being a sexual being."

It's what Bear told me, and I had no trouble believing him. The same had been true for the dancers in my club. The ones who loved it lasted longest.

"Huh," the boy says, frowning slightly.

"Why are you not up onstage performing rather than doing behind-the-scenes work? You move like a dancer."

Pain flashes over his face before he composes himself again. "I'm on the waiting list."

"I don't understand. I bet you're better than most of the guys out there. Some of them were clearly not selected because of their sense of rhythm."

He shrugs, but it's anything but casual. "I'm not the body type they're looking for. Their main audience consists of women, and women don't tend to go for a super gay, twinky guy like me. They want the big, strong men, the hairy bears with the rippling muscles and the ass that will make them wet their panties, or the slick, smooth guys whose chests feel so good when they're allowed to touch them. Me? I'm only attractive to gay men...and not that many of them show up here. They have one twink in the lineup, so until he quits, I'm on the waiting list."

The bitterness and anger are thick in his expression and

voice. And as much as I hate it, I can use it to my advantage. "So set up a meeting with me. You can see the studio, decide for yourself that we're legit. We'll discuss doing a trial video for me, for Kinky Boys. Just to see if you'll like it. I can promise you two things. One, you will always have the final say in who we pair you up with, so if you don't like whoever I pick for you, you can veto."

His look changes, and for the first time I see a spark of interest in his eyes. Trust issues. Totally called that one right.

"And the second thing I can promise is that I take good care of my boys." I have to swallow back the wave of emotions that rises in me. I've said those words so many times, and I've always meant them, but now more than ever. What happened in New York can not ever happen again. "I pay you well, and I pay on time. If you sign a contract with me, I'll go to the mattresses for you. We appreciate you for who you are, and you can be yourself. No hiding, no shame. Ever. You wanna show up with makeup and painted nails? Fine by me. You know what I'm saying?"

He nods. "I hear ya. But there's one thing you're not mentioning. The kink part. I get a say in that too? Like, what kind of kink I wanna do?"

I could slap myself so hard right now. The kink part is such an integral part of my life that I sometimes forget it's not like that for others. "Of course. Everything we do is consensual, so we'll never make you do anything you don't want. We're hoping to explore a wide range of kinks, both for absolute beginners and people who have experience with it. We'll talk about what you would like."

He studies me for a few seconds, then turns to Joey, who's been silently standing beside me that whole time. "Is he legit?" he asks him.

Joey nods. "Yeah. I haven't worked for him long, but I used to work for Ballsy Boys, and—"

"You worked for Ballsy Boys?" the boy interrupts him. "Like, the real Ballsy Boys?"

"Yeah. I was their head cameraman for ten years. Look on the credits, and you'll find my name, Joey Finch. And Kinky Boys is officially partnered with Ballsy Boys. Bear, the owner of Ballsy Boys, and Hunter here are good friends."

"I love the Ballsy Boys," the boy says. "Pixie is, like, my spirit animal or something."

Joey laughs, and I love the sound of it. It makes me realize I've never heard him laugh like this, so genuine and carefree. "Everybody loves Pixie. It's impossible not to like him."

He studies me again for a bit, then sticks out his hand. "I'm Ian. I'm officially interested, so let's talk."

My smile is broad as I shake his hand. "You have my card. Contact me. If you don't, I'll assume you've reconsidered, and I won't bother you again. It was nice meeting you, Ian."

Ian looks at the card in his left hand, then takes his wallet from his back pocket and carefully puts it in there. "Likewise. You'll hear from me."

"Thanks for helping me out there," I say to Joey as we walk outside, past a long line of giggling women who are waiting to take pictures with the performers.

"Sure thing," he says. "Can I ask you something, though?"

I stop so we can talk here. Once we're outside on The Strip, it will be impossible in the throngs of people looking to have a good time. "Shoot."

"Why did you pick him? You could've approached any of the dancers, but you picked him."

It's a fair question but one that's not so easy to answer. "He reminds me of Pixie," I say. "And knowing how insanely popular that boy is, I figured Ian would be a great choice. But..." I struggle to find words. This shouldn't be as hard as I make it, so why can't I come right out and say it? "He looks like someone who could be my boy. He's my type. Not that I would ever start anything with him, but he's someone who could've been my boy had we met under different circumstances."

It's the whole truth, so why didn't I feel even a spark of sexual attraction to Ian? Am I working so hard I can't summon the energy for sex anymore? I was hard watching the show, though, and I certainly reacted when that guy rubbed his thong-clad ass against my crotch.

"Oh, okay," Joey says with a strange look on his face.

I guess we've reached the limit of what he wants to know as a straight man. I can't blame him for that, and yet I'm weirdly irritated. I don't know what the hell is wrong with me, but this needs to stop. I need my head in the game. The big head, not the little one. And the sooner I determine what's causing me to be off my game, the better. This shit is getting annoying.

4

DADDY

I stretch myself, and several joints pop. That's what happens when I sit in the same position for too long: my body gets stiff and not in the good way. The fact that it never used to be a problem up until a few years ago is something I'd rather not contemplate. Age has become a bit of a sensitive subject for me.

The good news is that I've gone over all the numbers again with Bear, and he agrees that it looks solid. We've decided to go live with the first video a month from now, and I'm hopeful we can shoot a second one before that happens. I found a couple, a Dom and his cute boy, who are willing to do a few shoots for us. One of the boy's kinks is exhibitionism, so that makes them a good fit. They aren't interested in coming on as regulars, but if they'll honor the three shoots we agreed on, I'll be happy as a clam.

Whether we'll be able to shoot depends mostly on Joey, who's doing final checks on the setup right now. His advice has been invaluable, and I've rarely worked with someone easier than him. Oh, he knows how to put his foot down when it matters, but he's been more than flexible in every other aspect.

I make my way down to the studio part of the building. I was finally able to terminate the lease on that office space and move into what will be our studio. The sign I ordered hasn't arrived yet, but it will look amazing once it's hung on the front of the nondescript building. It has zero charm, but I'm still beyond proud as I look around.

Joey must be in the back room because I hear him muttering. "What's up?" I ask as I step in. Joey's bent over, about to lift a heavy equipment crate off the floor. "Wait!" I order sharply.

He jerks in surprise, then lets go of the crate and rights himself. "Something wrong?" he asks with a puzzled expression.

"You're lifting it with your back. You have to use your core and legs. When you do it like that, you could get yourself some serious back pain."

Joey looks at me as if he's not sure I'm serious or not. "You do realize I've been doing this for a while, right? Lifting crates is not new."

"Then you've been doing it wrong for years," I insist. "Look, here's how you should do it."

I gently push him aside, then bend my knees and lift the crate, engaging my core, my legs, and my arms. "Where does this go?"

Joey points at the heavy-duty, metal storage rack that lines the wall. "On the bottom to the left."

When I turn around after putting the crate in its place, he looks at me funny. "That's how you do it," I say, feeling strangely self-conscious from the way he studies me.

"Okay."

I shake off the weird sensation. "Where are we at?"

"I checked all the cables and only found one that had a break, but it's right near the end, so I can shorten it and still use it. The cameras and lights are all tested, and we're good to go. I'm not entirely happy with the arrangement of the set yet as I still get some annoying shadows, but we're close."

"Good." I observe him as he puts the last crate in its place, lifting it the way I showed him. I choke back the *good boy* that's on my lips. Damn, that shit is hard to let go of.

Joey looks a bit haggard. His face is way too pale for someone who lives in Vegas. Am I running him ragged?

"Have you eaten yet, Joey?" I ask, and his head shoots up.

"I had lunch?"

He makes it sound like a question, and it's kind of adorable. I must intimidate him more than I realized. "Dinner. I'm talking about dinner."

"Oh. No, I haven't."

For anyone else, that sentence would've been followed by the question "why are you asking," but Joey doesn't ask. Instead, he watches me, putting the ball back in my court.

"Let's go grab a bite. You look like you need a good meal."

"Yes, Daddy," he says, and my mouth drops open.

My heart rate jumps up at that word he used so casually. Does he have any idea what it means to me? What it does to me to be called that? What is he saying here? God, I'm so confused. "What?"

His cheeks redden. "You're called Daddy, right? That's your nickname. Daddy. Pixie told me. And you act like one, being all concerned and telling me to eat and how to lift properly. That was all I was saying."

Oh. Right. Like *that*. He's not wrong, but it still threw me that he'd call me that. Maybe it was his way of teasing? Or of showing that he knows about what I like and that he is okay with it? It could also be a subtle way to tell me to back off and mind my own fucking business. Or maybe I'm an idiot who's reading way more into a simple word than I should? I'm gonna go out on a limb and declare that last option the most likely one.

"I'm sorry. I didn't mean to treat you like a boy. Force of habit, I guess."

Joey shrugs. "I don't mind."

I frown. That's not what I expected him to say. "You don't?"

"Why would I? It's kinda sweet, isn't it? And it's not like I'm not used to it with Bear. That man was a Daddy long before he and Pixie got together."

His voice holds a dreamy undertone that would have made me wonder if I wasn't so damn sure he was straight.

"I'm glad you can appreciate their relationship."

He looks at me as if I'm saying something weird. "Those two are perfect for each other, and if Bear hadn't been such a stubborn ass, they would've been together months ago. Why would I not appreciate that?"

It feels to me like we're talking in circles, so I decide to drop it. "Let's go eat. What kind of food do you like?"

"I eat everything. No allergies, few things I don't like, no issues with anything."

Him being so compliant makes it easier, and yet something about his words strikes me. Everyone has food they love. People may love one kind of food or a few select things, but they always have a preference. Like, I love a good steak, and I'm super appreciative of great Mexican food, but if you ask me what I'd prefer here, I'd pick steak. My preference for steak over tacos is a small one, but it still exists. Why wouldn't Joey have one?

"Okay. So what are you in the mood for?"

He shoves his hands into his pockets. "I've only been back here for a little while, so I have no idea of good restaurants and shit. Why don't you pick?"

In that moment, I realize two things. The first is that Joey likes someone else to be in charge, at least outside of his work. It's not even that he doesn't mind me Daddy-ing him and making decisions for him. He *likes* it, and I'm not sure he's even aware of it.

The second thing is that *I* like it. You'd think that as a Daddy, I always prefer people around me who let me run the show, but that couldn't be further from the truth. In the bedroom and in my relationships? Hell yes, I'm in charge. No doubt about it. But in life in general, I love having friends who push back, friends who are just as dominant as me or somewhere in between. It keeps me sharp. And humble.

But Joey surrendering control to me like this? I like it. Way more than I should. Maybe I'm much more desperate for a new boy or a good round of sex than I thought because I've reached a new low when I project my Daddy issues onto my new, straight cameraman, who's practically my age. He's super nice, and even though he's not the type I usually go for, I find myself thinking about him in a way I shouldn't. Not about a straight employee.

I gotta get laid, man. This is ridiculous.

JOEY

WHY THE HELL did I call Hunter *Daddy*? Maybe because he was doing that thing Bear always seemed to do for Pixie—helping, *caring*—but that doesn't explain why it felt so oddly right on my tongue. He looked so shocked when I said it, but there was an undercurrent of something else in his expression too, something I've grown familiar with through my years of filming porn. It turned him on. The thought warms my insides in an unexpected way, and for a second, I pull up the image of Pixie cuddled on Bear's lap, but instead of Pixie and Bear, it's Hunter and me. My breath catches, and an unfamiliar feeling blooms in the pit of my stomach.

"Why don't we take my car," he suggests, and I realize I was in a complete daze as we made our way out to the parking lot.

"Oh, yeah, sure," I agree, changing course to follow him toward his sleek, black Lexus.

He doesn't get in right away. Instead, he rounds the front of the car and opens the passenger door for me. I must not hide my surprise well because he gives me an apologetic smile.

"Habit," he explains. Even though I know he doesn't mean anything by the gesture, something about it stokes the heat in my stomach again.

"It's nice, thank you," I say quietly, clearing my throat and then slipping into the car. I half expect him to reach in and pull my seat belt across my lap for me, but instead, he simply closes the door gently and gets in on the driver's side.

My hands shake slightly as I buckle myself in. In my forty years, I've never felt anything like this, and I can't decide if I like it or not, let alone what it means.

"I'd kill for a steak right about now. Sound good?" he checks as the engine purrs to life. I nod, and my stomach growls in agreement. He was right. I haven't been paying all that much attention to my meals. Between spending time with my mom, checking in on my dad, keeping my aunt from getting too down, and helping to set up the studio, there hasn't been much time left over.

When we reach the restaurant, a strange part of me is tempted to take my time unbuckling in hopes that Hunter will open my door for me again, but the rational part of my mind realizes how silly that impulse is, so I hurry to extricate myself and get out of the car before that happens.

When we enter the restaurant, the hostess's eyes go wide. I glance over at Hunter beside me and take him in for a few seconds—shoulders squared, well dressed, a friendly smile on his lips—he's an extremely attractive man. I certainly can't blame her for enjoying the view.

She shows us to our table, blushing and smiling at him the entire way.

"You should consider starring in one of the first videos," I say with offhand amusement once she leaves us alone.

His eyebrows go up, and he chuckles. "What makes you say that?"

"You have the kind of presence people can't help being attracted to. I guarantee people would subscribe to the site in droves if there was a thumbnail of you bending some cute boy over."

Hunter's expression darkens briefly, and he gives a sharp shake of his head. "It's not a good idea. Besides, we're going to end up with so many gorgeous men signed on to be Kinky Boys I'll look like no more than an old man who's past his prime."

I snort a laugh. If he thinks *this* is past his prime, he must've had people literally falling at his feet at one point.

"I'm guessing Ian called?"

"Ian called," he confirms. "He's coming in for an official sit-down next week. I figure we probably need three more full-time models to start with, and then we can build up from there?"

"Four is a decent number of regular guys to launch with. That's eight different pairings, plus you can mix and match for some multipartner scenes. That'll give you at least a few months' worth of videos, more if you work in some one-offs like you've already got scheduled."

He nods, his eyes fixed on me as he listens. There's something intense about his attention, like he's pinning me in place with it. I feel like I need to say something really important to earn it, but the pressure of it makes my throat go dry, and words flee from my brain.

"I guess that means we'll need a few more scouting missions," he concludes when I'm finished.

"Have you tickets for more shows?" I tease.

"No, but I do have some thoughts on a few more places we can scope out possible hidden talent."

"Do tell."

"I think it'll be more fun to surprise you." He grins and shoots me a playful wink.

"Now you're having too much fun playing with the straight dude," I accuse, and his eyes do that heating thing again like when I slipped and called him Daddy back at the studio.

"Can't blame a guy," he replies.

I open my mouth to volley back another teasing response when the waiter shows up to take our order.

"Oh shoot, I forgot to look at the menu," I say with a laugh, flipping it open to peruse the options.

"Would you be offended if I ordered for you?" Hunter asks. I whip my head up to look at him.

"Oh, um…"

"You said you're not picky? No allergies?" he checks, and

I nod. "We'll both have a top sirloin, medium, twice baked potato, and grilled asparagus." He hands the menus to the waiter, and I continue to stare at him for several seconds in an awed stupor.

"Thank you."

"My pleasure. I've been here a few times since moving to the city. Their top sirloin is heavenly."

"So, why Las Vegas? I can't imagine it would've been difficult to open a porn studio in New York."

His expression darkens again, this time even more stormy than before, a tormented look flickering in his eyes. "Sometimes you just need a change of scenery."

"I get it."

I don't really, but it's obviously a sore subject, so I'm not going to push for details he's clearly not comfortable giving.

We spend the rest of dinner discussing safer subjects like Bear and how I came to work in gay porn. By the time we pull into the parking lot at the studio so I can pick up my car several hours later, I have a grin that won't quit and a pleasant feeling in my chest.

"Thanks for feeding me, and thanks for a nice evening of avoiding my problems," I say as I climb out of the car.

"Anytime," he says. "Drive home safe, and I'll see you tomorrow. We've got a scene to film in no time. We've gotta get this place in top shape."

"It will be," I assure him. "I'll see you tomorrow."

5

DADDY

Being a business owner, at least in this stage, involves lots of begging and pleading. Now don't get me wrong. I love me some begging and pleading...but not when I'm the one doing it. Give me a sweet boy on his knees for me, begging me to let him suck me off; that's heaven. Burying myself up to my balls in said sweet boy while listening to him pleading to be allowed to come? Even better.

But fuck, I hate it when *I'm* the one doing the begging and pleading. I've contacted about everyone from New York —the people who are still willing to talk to me after what happened—but the response so far has been lukewarm. It's not that people don't want to be involved, but Las Vegas is a world away from New York City. They're happy to visit, do a scene or two, but no one wants to stay.

I should be grateful they're offering to help in the first place, but man, this is becoming so much harder than I had anticipated. I turn to the last number I jotted down to try. Marshall. Fingers crossed.

"Well, there's a name I haven't seen pop up on my caller

list for a while," Marshall says in his deep voice as he picks up the phone. "How have you been, stranger?"

I exhale at the warmth in his tone. It's been hard to tell who my real friends were, and I've had some people turn on me that I never saw coming. "It's been rough for a while, but I've found solid footing again."

"I'm glad to hear that. You had me worried there, friend."

"Thank you. I'm sorry I haven't been in t—"

"Don't apologize," Marshall cuts me off. "You deal with shit like that however you need to. I just hope you knew I was here had you needed me..."

As openings go, it can't get better than this. "Actually, I was calling you to ask you for a favor. Or more accurately, to approach you with a business opportunity."

"Hold on. Let me grab my tea, and we'll talk."

Marshall and his tea. The man is as particular and passionate about it as I am about my coffee. I hear some rustling, then the sound of liquid being poured. More rustling and then Marshall's back, though a slight change in sounds indicates he probably put in earbuds so he could talk hands-free.

"All right. Talk to me."

I take a deep breath. Here we go once more. God, I hope I don't have to resort to begging again. "I don't know if you heard it through the grapevine, but I'm starting a gay porn studio that will focus on kink. In Las Vegas."

Marshall whistles between his teeth. "That's a ballsy move."

I'm pretty sure he chose that word deliberately. "It's a partnership with Ballsy Boys, actually. Bear, the owner, and I go way back. He's an investor in my studio, which is called Kinky Boys, and he's advising me."

"Good. That means you're approaching it fair and square. I like that. Continue."

"I'd love to hire you as a consultant."

He lets out a low hum. "A consultant, huh?"

My shoulders sag a little. "I want everything to be on the up and up. My goal is to show that kink is not only fun and sexy but also that it should be done safely and consensually."

"You don't need consultants for that. Hunter, you've been in this business longer than I have. You're, what, ten years older than me? You've seen and done pretty much everything there is when it comes to kink. Why the hell would you need me for?"

I'll never be able to let it go, will I? Every time I think I'm finally free, it comes right back to bite me in the ass. "Because I need formal proof that someone else has signed off on it and not just me. My word doesn't mean that much anymore, Marshall. My reputation is tarnished. Forever."

"Here in New York maybe," Marshall says. He's never been one to sugarcoat it, and I appreciate his no-BS attitude. With him, you always know where you stand. "But it was a local incident, Hunter. It's not like the whole country knows what happens or even the whole kink community."

Bile rises in my throat. "You'd be surprised how far that news has traveled."

Marshall clicks his tongue. "It was an accident. An unfortunate accident that was not your fault despite how it got twisted and spun by his family."

"That's what I was certain of at first. Until I heard the other version so many times that I started doubting myself. I don't know anymore, but frankly, it doesn't matter either. Legally, the case is closed. Dismissed. Emotionally, well, we both know that's gonna take a while."

"That's why you moved to Vegas," Marshall says, and his tone is understanding.

"I needed a fresh start."

"Seems to me Vegas is as good a place to find one as anywhere else. It's a long way from New York, man."

"That was the whole point. Plus, Nevada looks kindly upon the type of business I want to run, so there's that. It was either this or LA, and that was too close to Bear. Or Florida, but that's a hell no from me. I can't deal with the humid heat eight months out of the year. I'll take desert heat, thank you very much."

Marshall chuckles. "Dude, you don't have to sell me. So what would being a consultant look like?"

"I want you to approve the script before filming, coach all participants in a scene and go over it with them beforehand so they know exactly what to do and what not to do, and for the first few scenes, I'd love for you to be there while we're shooting as well."

Marshal whistles again. "That's not a job I can do from here."

"No."

This is where everyone else lost interest, and I'm fully expecting Marshall to do the same. People won't just drop everything and move across the country, apparently. Who knew? Well, to be fair, I did because if you'd asked me two years ago to leave New York, I would've laughed you out of the room. How the times have changed and the mighty have fallen and all that.

"It's a paid position, I hope?" Marshall asks, and I sit up straight. Is he considering it?

"Yes. We can talk about your salary, and I have some connections here to get you an apartment."

"Hmm," he says noncommittedly. "And do you have a crew assembled yet? Boys? Equipment?"

"It's all in progress, and things are looking good," I assure him, but he laughs.

"I see you've adopted the business lingo already. That was code for 'it's all still up in the air, but I'm hopeful I'll have something resembling a studio when you arrive.' Right?"

I chuckle sheepishly. I should've known better than to try and fool Marshall. He's one of the best Doms I know and sharp as a tack. The man misses little when it comes to social cues and both verbal and nonverbal signals, so why I even thought I could pull the blinds over his eyes is beyond me.

"I don't have all the practical details arranged yet, but the website is good to go, and I have a phenomenal first video that's bound to go viral."

I think of the shoot Bear did for me with his boy, Pixie. It was hot as fuck, that first of all, but it had more than that. Chemistry. Love. Actual feelings. That's not surprising because anyone can see how much those two are in love, but I hadn't expected it to come across that well on video. It's made my heart ache for a boy of my own, but I've pushed that down.

"I have one boy who's signed a contract, so that's a start. A few more are considering it."

"I may know someone who's interested," Marshall says, and my ears perk up.

"I like the sound of that."

"He's a Dom, frequent visitor of a club in Vegas. He goes by the name of Harley. I did a demonstration with him once, and he's a good guy. Experienced, responsible. Want me to approach him? See if he's interested?"

"Yes, please. That would be amazing. Thank you."

Marshall hmms. "Anyway, you said you have one boy and a few who are considering signing."

"I also have an amazing cameraman," I say, and my belly warms as I think of Joey. "He's worked for Ballsy Boys for years, and he's the best."

"At his job or at extracurricular activities?" Marshall teases.

I roll my eyes, which he can't see, obviously, but it still gives me satisfaction. "At his job, asshole. He's my age and about the furthest thing from a sweet boy you can imagine. In other words, very much not my type. Besides, he's straight."

I don't even know why I add that last bit. Maybe because I still find it hard to believe a straight man would want to do this job? I mean, he could've easily gotten a position with a straight porn studio, what with his credentials and all.

"He's what?" Marshall asks, and it feels good he reacts the same way I did.

"He's straight," I say, not even bothering to hide the smugness.

"You're fucking kidding me."

"Nope. We even went to a gay strip show last week, and I swear, he didn't bat an eye. I was practically drooling when one of those boys dropped his barely clad, round ass in my lap, grinding down hard, but he only blushed when it happened to him. He never touched, never got excited, never so much as cheered when they took their clothes off. I'm telling you, the dude is straight."

Marshall is quiet for a few seconds. "You know, I'm not gonna call you a liar because I know you're not making shit up, but a straight man working in gay porn for that long? I'll need to test my gaydar in person. You got yourself a consultant, boss."

My joy at his acceptance of my proposal is only tempered by the way he worded it. "You're telling me you're only accepting the job to check out my straight cameraman?"

Marshall's laugh is booming. "No, man. Though I will admit I'm more than a little curious." Then he sobers, and his voice changes. "Like you, I could use a fresh start, so I'll give you six months. I can sublease my apartment here. If I don't like it, I can move back."

Hearing he's only joking about Joey is a relief. At least we've got that straight, though why it matters, I can't figure out. Maybe I'd better not think about that for too long. I don't know why Marshall wants a fresh start, and I'm not gonna ask. He'll tell me if he wants to. "Welcome to the team, man. Glad to have you."

6

JOEY

I've checked and rechecked every single camera and light half a dozen times to make sure everything is ready for our first official shoot at Kinky Boys studios. The first video we filmed with Pixie and Bear a few months back was technically filmed in LA at Ballsy Boys, even though it's being released as a Kinky Boys exclusive, so I consider this our maiden voyage.

I didn't expect to be nervous about filming today, but the urge to impress Hunter is stronger than I'd ever admit out loud.

"Everything looking good?" Hunter asks.

"I think we're set to go," I answer. "Everything good over there, Silas?" I check, and he gives me a thumbs-up from behind his camera. Hunter hired Silas as the other cameraman, and I've been training him for the past few weeks. He has some experience and a degree to back it up, but this is his first time shooting porn, which means he has a lot to learn about the industry specifics. He's a good guy, though, if maybe a little intense at times.

"I'm going to bring Nick and Benny in, then, to check out

the set and get comfortable before we start filming," Hunter says.

"Sounds good. If they want to hang out on the bed and get comfortable, I can double-check all the framing."

"You got it." He pats me on the shoulder, and just like the last time, I lean into the touch a little more than I probably should before his hand disappears, and he turns to get our stars for the day.

A few minutes later, both men make their way onto the set. Hunter explained to me earlier that Nick is the Dom and Benny is his boy. He said shooting this scene is Nick's birthday present to his boy. Obviously my only exposure to any kind of kink so far has been Bear and Pixie, but Nick and Benny definitely fit the mold I had in my mind. Nick is a large man, tall and broad-shouldered with a few wrinkles around his eyes that show his age and a sprinkle of gray in his short beard. Benny is petite and pretty with full lips and wide eyes.

My mind fills with that image I conjured of Hunter and me, and a stone sits heavy on my chest. What a silly thing for me to think of. Even if I could see the appeal of being like *that* with Hunter or someone like him, surely they'd all prefer boys like Benny, like Pixie, like Ian. That's what a boy is supposed to look like, and I'm a middle-aged man with wrinkles and gray hair of my own.

They sit down on the bed, and I shake off my melancholy thoughts to check the framing. The set looks incredible, even better than the bedroom set at Ballsy Boys. Hunter has several sound stages with different sets for various scenes, which will be a lot more efficient than having a whole crew to put up and tear down new sets every week.

Nick reclines on the bed, and Benny cuddles up next to him, looking at his Dom with adoring eyes. I watch them through the camera lens for a few seconds as Nick brushes Benny's hair back and presses a gentle kiss to his forehead. My heart beats a little faster at the sweet gesture.

After so many years filming porn, I've become more convinced than ever that sex isn't as exciting as most people seem to find it. It's nothing but the sweating, grunting mechanics of achieving orgasm. My right hand has worked just fine for that all my life, generally with less mess and less aggravation than doing it with a partner. But as Nick captures his boy's lips, his strong hand resting around Benny's throat while they kiss slowly, the intimacy between them hits me hard.

I swallow around the lump forming in my throat and pull my attention away from the scene in front of me, glancing around for Hunter.

"We, um, might want to get started before they get too carried away," I suggest, clearing my throat and gripping the camera stand a little harder than necessary.

Hunter chuckles and shakes his head. "Good call. Hey, Nick, we're going ahead before we miss the good stuff."

"Good because my filthy boy has no patience whatsoever. Do you, boy?" he rumbles, dragging his nose along Benny's cheek.

Benny shakes his head. "No, Sir."

Nick scoops up his boy, places him at the foot of the bed with his button-down shirt hanging open to expose his smooth chest, and kneels behind him. I signal to Silas, and we start rolling.

I zoom in on Nick's hand wrapped loosely around Benny's throat, tilting the boy's head back so he can kiss him. Their tongues meet, and even from that close shot, there's no doubt about who's leading the kiss.

Panning out a little, I drag the frame along Benny's body,

following the path of Nick's hand as he caresses his boy's chest, then dips down to tease the waistband of his underwear, never quite slipping his hand inside but making Benny squirm all the same. His erection fills his underwear, the bulge jerking as Nick twists his nipple, drawing a muffled moan from the boy.

I keep the camera shots tight, inviting the viewer into the intimacy between the two of them, making it feel like they're part of the scene. Scenes like this between a real-life couple make my job almost too easy. Viewers eat this stuff up—the filthy, whispered words, the familiarity of the touches they share. Maybe that proves that there are more people out there like me than I thought, craving closeness more than simply the act of fucking.

Nick lifts Benny up, manhandling him into another position, and it starts to make a little sense to me why a Dom would like their sub to be small like that. No one could pick me up and toss me onto the bed like a sack of potatoes, and I can't imagine someone wanting to. I could fit on a lap, though, and I think I might be good at following directions.

Where are these thoughts even coming from?

I shake my head to clear them and focus on the scene again, pulling the framing back to get both men in the shot as Nick spreads Benny's ass cheeks to expose his tight, pink hole.

"Such a dirty boy, aren't you?" Nick growls, and Benny whines in agreement as Nick pushes his thumb into the tight pucker.

I'm sure all these strange musings about kink are simply because I'm surrounded by it now. Who wouldn't start to question themselves when overnight nearly everyone they know is into some kind of kink? Then again, I never had a big gay crisis or anything when suddenly everyone I interacted with was gay.

"Daddy," Benny gasps, and that confusing heat is back.

Keeping my camera steady, I spare a glance in Hunter's direction. He's watching the scene with interest, his arms folded over his broad chest and a slight bulge pressing against the front of his jeans.

Daddy

These two are gorgeous together, and I watch with a mix of arousal and jealousy, my cock hard in my jeans but my heart aching. It's clear how close they are. They share that same intimacy Bear and Pixie had in their shoot, and if Joey and Silas do their job well, that should translate beautifully on camera.

God, I miss this. Not just having a boy of my own, though it's been a while. I haven't even dared to think about another boy since Lex. And I shouldn't because even though I do my damnedest not to think about him and everything that happened, that doesn't mean I'm stupid enough to believe I'm fine. I'm not. At some point, I need to deal with this and work through it somehow, but for now, denial works perfectly, thank you very much.

Anyway, it's not having a boy I miss most. Or even the sex, although I will admit I haven't gotten any for some time now... and come to think of it, this has been my longest *drought* ever. No, it's the intimacy. What these two share is far more than sex, more than a kink. It's intimacy and in their case, love.

Nick now has his thumb buried in Benny's hole, and the

boy is writhing against him shamelessly, seeking more. "Mmm," Nick purrs. "My sexy, dirty boy. You like having something in your pretty hole, don't you?"

He slowly drags his thumb out, then pushes it back in. He told us beforehand that he loves to take it slow, and I assured him that he could and he should. We can edit out whatever we need to speed it up if we want, but honestly, so far, it's been mesmerizing to watch.

"Daddy..." Benny pants. "More, Daddy, please..."

"You haven't earned Daddy's cock yet, have you?"

Nick's tone is deceptively velvety, but I don't think Benny is fooled even for a second. The boy knows his Dom way too well.

"No, Daddy."

"What do you need to do to earn Daddy's big cock?"

Benny's eyes flutter as he sinks down onto that big thumb one more time, but then he lifts himself off and scrambles to his feet. He drops to his knees, and a quick check tells me Joey is on it, following him close with the handheld camera. As Joey sinks to his knees as well, he pushes his denim-clad ass back, and damn, the man knows how to fill a pair of jeans. He's no twink, but his body is strong, and that ass is just begging to be fucked.

I mentally sigh and focus on the ass that *will* get fucked today. Benny spreads his legs wide, offering us a tantalizing view of his perfectly shaped butt and that hole that's practically screaming to be filled. By now, my cock throbs, and I palm it briefly. I know what will be on my schedule after this: a five-minute appointment with my right hand. If I even need that long.

Benny's fully devoted to his job: making love to his Daddy's cock, and the boy has one talented mouth. I'm amazed Nick lasts as long as he does, but maybe he's trained himself.

"Mmm, such a sweet mouth you have," Nick praises his boy. "Such a good boy you are, worshiping your Daddy's cock."

Benny makes an unintelligible mumble, then the lovely sound of someone choking on dick. Call me mean, but I love hearing that. That wet gurgle, that quiet gasp, it's such a damn turn-on. Then again, I'm partial to seeing my cum drip out of a boy's mouth as well, especially if his eyes are still watery and he's drooling all over himself. Messy? Sure. But also hella sexy.

"Everyone will see what a good little cocksucker you are, my sweet boy," Nick continues. "Spread those legs wide, baby. Let them all get a good view at your pretty pink hole."

Even from here, I see a blush spreading across Benny's body. Ah, the perfection of sweet humiliation kink, where a boy can't decide if he loves it or hates it, and all he knows is that it turns him on. That's undeniable here as well, as Benny's cock is trailing precum onto the floor in thick ropes. Nick told me his boy loves humiliation as much as exhibitionism, so this is a perfect treat for him.

Nick has finally decided he's had enough, and with a strong move, he lifts Benny off the ground and plants him on his lap. Apparently, the time for taking it slow has passed because he holds his cock with one hand as Benny lowers himself, making beautiful little gasps as he takes him in with ease.

My gaze wanders off to Joey, who's close enough to the pair to get beautiful shots but has enough distance so he's outside the frame of the two fixed cameras that are recording the scene from different angles. He moves with ease, almost like a dance partner following the lead of the male. Wherever Nick and Benny go, Joey is in step with his camera, never so in their face he hinders them or distracts them but always close enough to get a shot.

What goes through his mind when he films a scene like this? He seems so cool, unfazed, even a bit distant. He's focused, which makes sense 'cause he's on the job, but I can't read any emotion on his face. Does he like it? Is he neutral to it, like he claims to be? You'd have to be really, *really* straight to not get turned on by two people fucking right in front of you.

I've shot some glances at his groin—I know, highly inappropriate for a boss to look at his employee, but this is the porn industry, so it's not like normal work rules apply here anyway—but he doesn't appear to be turned on, or if he is, it doesn't show. Unlike me, and I make a mental note to either get down with the fact that I'll pop a boner every time I watch a shoot or start untucking my shirts. If my dick gets any harder, I'm worried my zipper won't even hold.

Joey could've made the same amount of money in straight porn. Hell, he's talented enough that he could've made the switch to Hollywood. So why didn't he? It wasn't for the money, that's for sure. Bear paid him well, but he could've made much more had he gone mainstream commercial. What was it about the Ballsy Boys that made him stay for so long despite being straight? I still can't figure it out.

The moaning on set increases, and it takes me a second or two to realize Nick and Benny are well on their way to their first orgasm. We'd said we'd take a break after that one, let them rest for a little bit, and then pick back up.

That's my cue to step back into my office. I don't need to see the second half of the shoot. I'm already aroused as fuck, even though I've been watching Joey more than the two lovebirds.

Clearly, my priorities need some adjustment. I need to get my head straight because I've been way too distracted lately.

7

DADDY

Joey is a fucking genius. I'm rewatching the scene we did with Nick and Benny, and it's amazing. Granted, the chemistry between those two made the whole shoot effortless, but the way Joey has captured it is nothing short of perfection.

The difference between his shots and the ones Silas did is noticeable. It makes zero sense, but the latter are more clinical. They feel distant. Pretty but emotionless. Somehow, Joey has not only captured their bodies but their souls, their love.

That, and there's a little jerk in Silas's feed during the cum shot. I guess he didn't see that coming. *Har har.* It's something Joey will train him in, I'm sure. I hate to be superficial, but that shot matters. A lot. It's the moneymaker, and missing that will make the whole shoot pretty much useless. Good thing Joey captured it beautifully for this scene.

If all our videos are gonna look like this one, we'll be a fucking hit, no doubt about it. This is pure gold. As soon as that thought hits me, so does the worry that's been my constant companion for the last two years. I had gold with Balls to the Walls as well, and look how that ended up. It was my happy place, the thing in my life I was most proud of.

I've never been in long-term relationships, never had a boy to call my own for more than a year or so. At some point, they all moved on. Most of the time, it was in good harmony. I don't do angry breakups. I hate all the drama. It's so petty. If my boy wanted to leave? I let him go. You can't hang on to someone who doesn't want to stay. It's never gonna work.

And even though the relationship with my parents and siblings is warm and cordial, they live in a completely different world than me. They're all straight, supportive of me being gay, but as plain as vanilla can get. I love them dearly, but they don't understand my world at all.

So my club was my thing, my accomplishment, my claim to fame, so to speak. I had a name, a reputation, and I was proud of it. People from all over the country came to my club because they knew what I stood for. And then it all crumbled right before my eyes.

What if it happens here again? What if what I'm building here will fall apart, just like it did before? All it took was one night, one session to destroy everything I had built. I'm not sure I can go through something like that a second time.

"Is something wrong?" Joey's voice is hesitant as he stands in the door of the editing room, a frozen still of the scene still up on the screens. "You look so serious that I thought maybe something went wrong with the scene or that you weren't happy with it."

I push down my self-doubt and sadness. "No, on the contrary. The scene is amazing, and I was just thinking to myself what a fucking genius you are."

Joey gives me a half-assed smile. "Okay. You didn't *look* like you were thinking that, though."

He's perceptive, I'll give him that. "I'm sorry. I was thinking that a few minutes ago, I promise, and then my thoughts wandered off to something far less happy, and I got a little sad. It has nothing to do with the scene or with you. You're so fucking talented."

It's like watching a flower bloom. The smile spreads across Joey's face like the sun appearing from behind the clouds, and oh my god, I'm turning into some sappy poet, for fuck's sake. I need to fucking stop this.

"Thank you. I'm so glad you're happy with it. I have to admit I thought it turned out great as well."

"I got lucky that you had to relocate here. It's Bear's loss, but you're gonna be the key asset for this studio. I can already tell."

Joey shuffles his feet, looking all kinds of flustered, but the joy on his face shows how much he appreciates the praise. If he were my sub, I'd use praise as a reward because it's easy to see how much it means to him. And we're back in territory I shouldn't venture in with him. What is it about him that gets under my skin?

"Thank you. I think I'm gonna like it here, and I love the setup of the studio. If you ask me, it's even better than the Ballsy Boys one, since it's more versatile." He snickers. "Look at me, making jokes like that. I sound like Brewer."

His joke relieves some of the tension in me, so I laugh with him. "He's a jester, that one, huh?"

"God, yes. He used to drive Tank crazy before those two

finally got together. For a while, I wasn't sure if Tank was gonna kill him or fuck him for real."

His eyes seem to stare at something far away. "I guess you miss them," I say softly.

He nods. "I do. My family was all here—not that I'm close with them—and other than a few guys from the film academy, I didn't have many friends. They became my family, I guess you could say. Bear was good at that, making us bond and feel close. He took care of us really well."

He's lonely. I don't know why it never registered with me, but he's lonely. Bear said something about him having to move back because of family circumstances, so I don't know what's going on, but he's adrift without the family he found in the Ballsy Boys. It makes my desire to hang out with him even stronger. He's a good guy, and I enjoy his company.

"Why don't we grab a bite together again? We might as well eat together rather than both eating on our own," I suggest.

Joey takes me in, his eyes roaming over my body from my head all the way down to my feet. There's something oddly intimate about that look. "I'd think you have more than enough boys available to share a meal with you. And *more*."

I smile as I shrug. "Maybe, but that doesn't mean I'm in the mood for that."

I should be after that scene I watched because up until a few minutes ago, I was horny as fuck. But for some reason, the thought of sharing a meal with Joey is far more attractive than the idea of scoring a hookup. Maybe I *am* getting old.

"Well, I'm not gonna say no to a meal," Joey says. "It sure as hell beats eating some takeout on my own. So, where are we going?"

Daddy

He's so adorable, the way he lets me decide. And he's probably not even aware of it. "I'm in the mood for Italian. How does a little carb-loading sound?" I pat my stomach. "I'll have to do a few hundred extra sit-ups tomorrow morning to burn it off, but it'll be well worth it."

Joey's gaze lingers on my abdomen, which, I'll admit, is framed rather nicely in my tight, gray shirt. A six-pack is a thing of the past for me, but I do work hard to stay in shape.

"I don't think you're gonna have a problem looking good," Joey says, his voice just a tad hoarse, and if that's not the strangest thing to say for a straight man, I don't know what is. Maybe it's because he's been hanging out with gay porn stars for so long because fuck knows the Ballsy Boys are flirty and have zero filter. I guess that if you're exposed to that for too long, you not only get used to it but start mimicking it. Is he aware of it?

"Thanks," I say lightly. "Pasta it is, then?"

"Sounds good."

Why am I so hyperfocused on everything Joey says and does? You'd think he was like a code or a puzzle I'm trying to crack. I've spent more time thinking about him than I have on anyone in a long time.

I keep mulling it over as we make our way to my car—I promised Joey I'd drop him off here again after dinner. Something nags at me, but I can't put my finger on it. I take a quick look sideways as we pull onto the freeway. Joey stares ahead, but he looks happy, relaxed. As if he enjoys my company and is looking forward to dinner.

I scoff mentally. Here I go again, giving meaning to a simple look. It's ridiculous. Why the hell am I so aware of him?

Oh god.

Oh, fuck no.

I've broken the one rule I vowed never to break, the one thing I know will lead to heartbreak.

I've become attracted to a straight man.

Fuck me sideways.

8
JOEY

I check the time and curse under my breath. We filmed a screen test for Ian and Harley today, and it ran a lot longer than I'd expected. So long, in fact, that now I'm not sure I'll have time to swing by my mom *and* pick up groceries for my dad. He's probably already hungry and sitting there without dinner, but I'll be cutting it close as it is with visiting hours at the care facility.

My stomach grumbles, reminding me I haven't eaten today yet either, and it's already after six at night, so god knows when I'll have time to get around to it.

"Silas, do you think you're good finishing up with the equipment? I hate to run out like this, but I've seriously gotta go."

"Yeah, no worries," he assures me, waving me off.

"Thanks, I owe you one." I turn to leave and nearly crash right into Hunter.

"Whoa, where are you off to in such a hurry?" he asks, steadying me with his strong hands on my shoulders.

"I've, um..." I bite my lip and step out of his grasp. "I have some responsibilities I need to see to," I answer as vaguely as I can manage. His eyebrows crinkle, his concern burrowing its way into my chest.

"Bear mentioned you moved back here because of your parents. Is everything okay?" he asks.

I sigh, and my shoulders sag, the weight of the past few weeks feeling like it hits me full force all at once. "Not really, but I don't have time to stand around and chat about it right now. I need to stop and see my mom before visiting hours are over, and I need to pick my dad up something for dinner and some groceries," I explain, then huff out a helpless sort of laugh. "Not that she'll remember if I'm not there, and I'm sure *he's* just waiting to cuss me out, but I'm all they have, so I have to do it."

The concern on his face etches even deeper. "You haven't eaten in more than eight hours, and you're clearly exhausted on top of it."

I give a weak, one-shoulder shrug, not correcting him that it's actually been more like twenty-four hours since I ate last. I never sleep well when things are stressful. Eventually, it'll all get easier. At least that's what I keep telling myself.

"I really do have to get going."

"I'll help. Give me something to do," he says, his tone leaving no room for argument.

"I don't know. I can't think about anything right now," I answer with frustration.

"All right, take a deep breath," Hunter coaches, his hands on my shoulders again. The weight of them is more comforting than I'd like to admit, even to myself. The smooth confidence and authority in his voice make me believe for a few seconds that I don't have to worry about anything because he has it all handled.

I do as he says, dragging in a long breath and holding it for several heartbeats before slowly letting it out.

"Good boy," he murmurs, and I suck in a sharp breath. "Sorry, habit," he says, an apologetic smile twisting on his lips. "Here's what we're going to do. You give me your dad's address, and I'll bring him what he needs. That way you can see your mom before guest hours are over without worrying about your dad. Then you're going to come over to my place, and I'm going to cook you dinner."

"You don't have to do that."

He fixes me with a stern look, and relief blankets me. I really *don't* have to worry about anything right now. Is this what it's like for Pixie all the time? Bear takes care of everything? No wonder he's so happy. It must feel nice, knowing there's always someone there to make sure things are okay. The longing is back full force, and it's all I can do not to throw myself against Hunter in gratitude, which is even weirder than the rest of this.

I clear my throat. "Okay, thank you, I appreciate it. I'll text you his address. But I'm serious. He's been an absolute beast since we had to put my mom in the memory care facility. He's bound to throw something or use some very colorful language."

"Don't worry about it. I'm sure I can handle him."

"All right, I truly do appreciate it."

"Don't mention it."

I pull out my phone and text Hunter the address, and then we both head out.

I manage to make it in time to spend half an hour with my mom. Today she thinks I'm my dad, which is both better and worse than being her dead brother. At least she thinks my dad is visiting, I guess, so that's something. Just before I get up to leave, I see a momentary flicker of lucidity. The confusion about why she's in a strange place instead of home with my dad is worse than her thinking I'm someone else by a longshot.

By the time I make it out to my car, my heart is heavy and my mood is at an all-time low. I pull out my phone and call Hunter.

"Hey, just left your dad's place."

"How'd that go?" I ask, almost afraid to know the answer. Although *I'm* the one my dad is mad at, so he may have been perfectly friendly to Hunter.

"When he first opened the door, he was a little prickly, but once he saw the pizza I brought him, he calmed down pretty quickly."

I chuckle, some of the weight on my shoulders easing. "And you dropped off groceries?"

"Yup, he's all set for the next week, and I gave him my number in case he ever needs something and can't get ahold of you."

"What?" My throat tightens. "You didn't have to do that."

"I don't know why you keep saying that," he says. "I don't mind helping. Some loads are too heavy for one person to carry alone. I didn't realize you were dealing with so much, and here I was piling all this stuff on you for Kinky Boys."

"I didn't mind. I'm having fun getting the studio off the ground," I assure him.

"You still need a hand," he says. "*And* you still need dinner, so get your ass over to my place so I can feed you."

My stomach gives a small flip, and I grin, more than a little glad Hunter can't see me through the phone. "Yeah, okay. I'll meet you there soon."

"Good. See you soon."

Daddy

. . .

Joey wasn't wrong about his dad. I didn't exactly lie to him, but I may have left out a few things. Joey doesn't need to know that his father was distinctly unpleasant when I showed up, though he did change his tune after I smothered him with kindness. I can kiss ass like you wouldn't believe when I want to, and this situation certainly called for it.

My boy has enough on his mind. And for fuck's sake, I need to stop thinking of him as my boy. He's not, even though he clearly needs a Daddy. He needs *me*.

I've never met anyone so desperate for care and affection as him. He's starving for it, and I'm not sure he even realizes it. Probably, on some level, but I doubt he grasps how big his need is. He would do so well in a Daddy-boy relationship... aside from that pesky little detail of him being straight.

I must admit I haven't seen any evidence of him trying to score a date or even a hookup with a woman. Granted, between the number of hours he's making for me and the care of his parents, he doesn't have much time left. And what little time he has, I have no trouble claiming for myself, even if I do it to make sure he's eating.

If he wants a relationship, he needs a Domme. A Mommy-type of Domme. They're not as prevalent as Daddy-Doms, but they exist. Come to think of it. I should take him to a straight club. I'm sure I could introduce him to some good people there. My reputation may be shot in New York, but I still have connections here that look on me favorably.

The doorbell interrupts my thoughts, and when I open the door, Joey stands there, hands in pockets, and with that way-too-pale face. "Hi," he says, giving a half wave.

"Come on in." I open the door wide for him, and he slips by me with a shy expression.

He's such a contradictory mix. When it comes to his work, he's confident, self-assured, and he'll put his foot down if he has to. I've seen and heard him joke around with the others, and he can take a good ribbing as much as he can dish it out. But once it's the two of us, he's different. Way shyer. More...submissive. Is it because I'm a Dom and he reacts to that, even unconsciously? It would make sense.

"Your apartment is nice," Joey says.

"If you really think that, I don't want to see where you live. This place is a shithole, but for the first year, I wanted something cheap in case it didn't work out with Kinky Boys."

"Of course it's gonna work out. That scene with Bear and Pixie is pure gold, you said yourself how hot Nick and Benny were together, and you have some great shoots lined up."

That's what I mean. If you saw him now, all fired up, his hands on his hips, you wouldn't know it was the same man who let me order his food, who loves it when someone takes care of him.

"You don't need to convince me, boy." This time I do say it on purpose, watching as confusion flits over Joey's face.

"I didn't mean to..." He looks insecure, as if he's afraid he somehow offended me.

"You're fine." More than fine, in fact, but I don't say that part out loud. "I love your faith in the company. Let's eat, though, before the food gets cold."

I've made a quick pasta salad, nothing fancy, but it does have real food and nutrients. Joey sits down across from me at my small dining table, and we're quiet as we eat.

"How was your mom?" I ask after a while.

Joey shrugs. "Like she always is. Confused. Today she thought I was my dad. Usually, she thinks I'm her dead brother, so that was a change of pace. But she's declining fast. I should've had her in that facility a long time ago."

"You did what you could," I say, my voice warm. "And you were in a tough position, what with your dad so vocally opposed."

He sighs. "He told you that, huh?"

"I got the lecture about how it was a shame you had taken her away and all that."

"She was a danger to herself and others. They picked her off the side of the freeway once. Did he tell you that as well? Completely lost, no idea who or where she was. If she hadn't had her wallet in her pocket, they wouldn't even have been able to call my dad."

"I know. Trust me, I've got the picture. Which I told your dad as well."

Joey looks up from his plate, then quickly chews to empty his mouth. "You did?"

"He needs to stop blaming you. Deep down, he knows it's not your fault."

Joey scoffs. "He sure as fuck knows how to hide that."

"He's grieving, Joey. Grieving for the wife he lost before she passed away. Grieving for the life they had together. Grieving because he's alone now, effectively a widower, even if his wife is still alive."

Joey slowly puts down his fork and knife. "He's never visited her. Not once."

"I'm not defending him, but have you considered how hard it must be for him to see her and not have her remember who he is? Maybe he wants to remember her the way she was, back when she was still healthy."

Joey lets out a shaky breath. "I've never looked at it like that."

"Were you close with them before she got sick?"

He shakes his head. "No. They were perfectly okay parents, and they supported me going to film school, but once I started working for Ballsy Boys, that was it. They couldn't understand why I would throw my life away like that—their words, obviously. They didn't outright reject me or shun me, but things cooled down considerably between us. I'd visit them, but it was purely out of obligation."

I push my empty plate back, my stomach pleasantly full. "I'm sorry. I'm not super close with my family, but I know they love me and they've accepted me, even though they don't understand my choices."

Joey lets out a huge yawn, then looks at me sheepishly. "Sorry. It's been a long day."

I rise from my chair, then walk over to him and pull his chair back. He looks at me funny as I gesture for him to stand up, but he does it anyway.

"I may have a crappy apartment, but I have the best damn couch on the planet. It's so comfortable that it's actually nicer than my bed, if a little less roomy. So why don't you settle on the couch and entertain yourself with some TV while I clean up and load the dishwasher? We can watch a movie after or chat for a bit, whatever you want."

Of course he agrees. That's the point I've been making all damn day long. The boy wants to be cuddled, to be taken care of, and I'd love nothing more than to apply for the job, but alas, I'll have to settle for the crumbs until his real Domme shows up.

And so I watch as Joey lowers himself onto the couch, the moan falling from his lips positively sinful. I don't even need to tell him to use the soft blanket draped over the back of the couch because he's already grabbed it and covers himself with it. Once he's found the remote and has set the channel to ESPN, I go back to the kitchen.

It takes me maybe ten minutes to clean up and empty and repack the dishwasher. I'm about to make my after-dinner Nespresso when I wonder if Joey wants one too. But when I walk into the living room, he's fallen asleep on the couch, and I sit down the chair opposite him to observe him for a bit.

How can someone be so stupid at my age? You'd think I'd know better, but here I am, investing my heart into a man who'll never want me the way I need him to. The smart thing to do would be to distance myself from him, but I can't do that. Not when it's so clear he needs someone to look out for him. *Yeah, keep telling yourself that*. Sigh.

I guess that despite knowing better, I'm content with crumbs for now. If that's all I can have, I'll take it.

9

JOEY

"Hey, Dad," I call out as I step into the small house I grew up in, the place my father still lives in, all alone now.

The only response I get is the sound of the television being turned up louder. Fuck me, I guess. I sigh and heft the grocery bag in my arm higher, closing the door behind me and heading into the kitchen to put away what I brought over. For over forty years, the man had my mother cooking every meal for him. I can only imagine how much he's struggling now that she's at the care facility.

I don't just mean food either, although that's the only thing I feel like I can help him with. I'm sure he's lonely too, but every time I drop by, he goes out of his way to either glare at me silently or find some project he suddenly needs to do urgently as a way to avoid me.

I know Hunter was right in saying that my dad is acting out because he's hurting over my mom, but it doesn't make the cold shoulder much easier.

I fill Dad's freezer with easy-to-heat meals and his refrigerator with lunch meats and a fresh gallon of milk. It should be enough to tide him over for the week. After that, I can stop by again with more supplies. Not that the man can't go to the grocery store himself, but I suppose it makes me feel better to know I'm doing something for him.

I wander into the living room and lean against the doorframe. I know he can see me in his peripheral vision, but he doesn't acknowledge me in any way.

"Hey, Pop, I dropped off some food for you. If there's anything special you want next week, let me know, and I can make sure to include it," I say, and he grunts. Hey, that's more than I've gotten in the few weeks I've been home. Maybe we're making progress. "I stopped by and saw Mom this morning too. She seems like she's enjoying herself. She was doing some kind of craft project with a few friends she's made there."

"She should be home with me," he growls. A complete sentence. That *is* progress.

"You know why she can't be anymore. I'm sure she'd love it if you visited, though. I can swing by and pick you up before my visit in two days if you want."

"I don't want to see her like that, stuffed away in some nursing home where they could be doing god knows what to her."

"They're really nice there. If you come see for yourself, I'm sure you'll feel better," I reason.

"I said no," he says through gritted teeth, picking up the heavy glass ashtray from the small table beside his chair and whipping it at the wall only a few feet away from me. I jump back, my heart hammering at how close that came. "Get the fuck out."

My hands are shaking as I pick up the ashtray and place it on the coffee table, far out of his reach.

"If you change your mind, you know my number," I say,

doing my best to keep the quiver out of my voice. "See you next week."

My whole body is still trembling as I climb into my car, and I take a few deep breaths to try to steady myself. I tilt my head back against the headrest and close my eyes, focusing on my breathing and getting myself under control.

After a few minutes, my heart rate returns to normal. I open my eyes and start the car. But before I can pull out of the driveway, my phone buzzes with a text.

HUNTER: Up for a little meet and greet with a potential Kinky Boy?

AS MUCH AS I want to go home and feel sorry for myself all alone in my apartment, helping Hunter vet a new prospect will probably do a lot more for my mental state.

JOEY: Sure. At the studio?
Hunter: No, one second. I'll send you the address

A FEW MOMENTS LATER, my phone buzzes again with an address. I'm not familiar with it, but it looks like it's several miles outside of the city, essentially in the middle of the fucking desert.

A short time later, I pull up in front of the large, nondescript building. It's impossible to tell what this place actually is. But if it's in the middle of nowhere like this, I'm guessing it's something too unsavory even for Vegas proper. Maybe a brothel?

Before I can get out of my car, Hunter is pulling up beside me. It's a little cool as I open my door and step out. People think of Vegas as always scorching hot, but once the sun goes down, it can get chilly quickly. He follows suit, getting out of his car and turning to grin at me over the roof of it.

"Glad you could make it."

"Yeah. Where are we exactly?"

"Ball and Chain," he says the name as if it should mean anything to me. It doesn't exactly sound like a brothel, but I'm no expert. "It's a kink club," he explains when I don't react.

"Oh." The single word comes out breathier than I would've liked. After my recent confusion around Hunter and while filming last week, I wonder if I should feel more reluctant to go inside. There's a strong chance I'll see something that will only mess with my head further, but I find myself excited anyway. Why, I have no idea, but the telltale flutter in my chest is unmistakable.

"Is this okay? If you're uncomfortable, I can do this myself," he says, moving toward me with concern crinkling his forehead.

"No, it's fine," I assure him. "Let's go."

I trail a few steps behind Hunter, who walks up to the door with his shoulders back and a confident swagger in his gait. He glances back every few steps to make sure I'm still behind him, offering me reassuring smiles that give me a little thrill each time. There's a front desk where we're supposed to sign in. Apparently, whoever we're here to meet had to put us on a guest list. Who knew these things were so official?

"I believe Harley James is waiting for you in the lounge. Enjoy your evening." The woman waves us through the inner door, and I increase the speed of my steps to stay close to Hunter, a shiver of trepidation creeping up my spine. God only knows what kinds of things I might see inside—whips, chains, blood...

My breath whooshes out of me, and I laugh quietly to myself as we step through the door to find a perfectly normal-looking lounge. At first glance, it could be any high-end club in the world, complete with large, comfortable booths and soft music playing from overhead speakers. It's only after observing the patrons for several seconds that the differences register. There are men and women in various states of undress, some wearing collars or even leashes, others kneeling or acting as tables or footrests.

My heart beats faster, and my stomach heats again in that same way that confused me last week. I'm starting to think this is how it's supposed to feel to *want*, to long for something. I look at Hunter, checking to see if he's noticed the change in me that feels so monumental, but he's scanning the room.

"There he is," Hunter says, putting a hand on my shoulder and leading me toward a man seated by himself off to the left side of the room.

I do my best to pull my head together before we reach him, getting into a professional headspace by assessing the man. He's handsome, clearly tall—obvious, even if he's seated—long dark hair pulled back in a ponytail. He lifts a drink to his lips, and I see a full-sleeve tattoo down his arm. Viewers will go absolutely wild for his bad-boy looks; that's a guarantee. He glances in our direction, studying us right back. There's an intense look in his eyes that makes me wish I had my camera so I could capture it.

"Harley?" Hunter asks. He stands and offers a hand.

"That's me. Marshall tells me you're called Daddy, but

I'm putting it out there right now that there's no way I'm calling you that."

Hunter chuckles. "I'm starting to wonder if I should change my moniker, since I can never get any other Doms to use it," he jokes before turning slightly to beckon me forward. "This is Joey. He's the head cameraman for Kinky Boys. He worked for Ballsy Boys studios before this, so he's kind of my right-hand man while we get everything up and running."

He puts a hand on the back of my neck and gives it the barest squeeze, sending warm sparks cascading over my skin. Does he realize what he's doing? Is the touch simply force of habit, or does it mean something more? Before I can think too hard about it, his hand is gone, and I'm left feeling cold.

"Joey? No nickname?" Harley teases, reaching out and shaking my hand.

"No nickname," I say, and we all sit down at the table. "Is Harley your given name or a nickname?"

He smirks and quirks an eyebrow. "Not much fun if I tell you."

So, he wants to play it a little mysterious. The viewers will certainly love that.

"Marshall spoke very highly of this project. I'd love to hear more about it," Harley says, and Hunter launches into his spiel about his vision for bringing realistic, safe kink scenes to viewers both experienced in the scene and those just becoming curious. Since I don't have much to contribute, I make myself useful watching Harley's body language while he talks with Hunter. He has the same air of authority and confidence that all the Doms I've met so far seem to radiate, but there's also an easy, open demeanor about him. He has a warm, comfortable laugh and doesn't seem to take himself too seriously. I'm not sure why Hunter needed me here because anyone can see the instant interest and enthusiasm he appears to have for the idea Hunter is trying to bring to life.

Since I'm clearly not needed, I let my attention wander, curiously absorbing more of the nuances of the club. While for the most part, everyone in the lounge area is behaving like anyone else out in public, the sound of distant moans and louder music catches my ear every so often. There are a number of doors off the main room, and I'm assuming far more interesting things happen behind the scenes.

Not that what's happening in the lounge isn't interesting in its own way. I sneak a peek at one of the subs kneeling on the floor a few feet away. He's looking up at the man seated beside him, his Dom I'm guessing, with a look of awe and adoration that I'm starting to recognize. But what catches my attention more than the look in his eyes is the man himself.

He's not a twentysomething boy with long eyelashes and a smooth body. He's a little round in the middle, and the hair on his chest has streaks of gray in it. There are laugh lines around his eyes, and his hair is just starting to thin. In spite of all that, his Dom reaches down and strokes his hair lovingly, an offhand acknowledgment of the man as he holds a conversation with someone else. It's...beautiful.

"Joey?" Hunter says my name with a hint of concern. I snap my attention away from the man and back to the conversation in front of me.

"Sorry, what?" I ask.

"I was commenting on your work," Harley explains with a smile. "I love the vision Hunter has, and with your artistry putting it on film, I have no doubt this is going to be something special to be part of."

"Oh, thank you. Daddy's been working hard, and I think this is going to be amazing once it all comes together," I agree, looking at Hunter and noticing how his eyes go wide at the slip of his nickname.

Was it a slip, though? I ask myself. Maybe I wanted to see how it felt on my tongue again. I'm still not sure of the final verdict.

"Great. Well, needless to say, I'm in. Why don't you email me a contract to look over, and we can go from there?" Harley says, standing up and offering Hunter his hand again. "And I hate to run off, but I have a scene I need to get to. I can't leave a sweet sub waiting." He winks.

"Of course. Don't let us keep you. I'll be in touch."

We say our good-byes, and I'm a little disappointed when Hunter stands so we can leave as well. I glance at the other man again quickly before returning my attention to Hunter.

"Can I ask you something?" I ask, even as my mouth starts to go dry.

"Sure, what's up?"

"I thought most subs were, um...like Pixie," I say, trying to come up with the right words. I flick my eyes over to the older man again, and this time Hunter follows my gaze, understanding dawning in his face.

"I'll admit, there does tend to be a bit of a bias toward young, pretty subs. But that doesn't mean that more mature subs don't exist. Just like with anything else, everyone has different tastes. Some Doms would much rather play with someone with experience."

A surprising amount of relief whooshes through me before another thought occurs. "But what if you're not young, but you're also not experienced as a sub?"

His eyebrows scrunch together, and his eyes bore into

me like he's trying to read my mind. "Joey, are you—" His eyes are a storm of emotions—surprise, tenderness, and unmistakable heat. In any other context, I would know exactly what that kind of hungry expression means. I've seen it enough, captured it hundreds of times on film. But surely Hunter can't want me that way? Not when he could have any boy in the world.

"For research," I cut him off. "If I'm filming kinkier stuff now, I figured I should understand the dynamics so I can do it justice." It's not a complete lie.

"Oh, that makes sense. I should've realized that. I can teach you about the basics of the lifestyle if that will help."

"Yeah," I answer, licking my lips and nodding quickly. "That would be great."

10

DADDY

I have another interview lined up, and this one, too, I owe to Bear, though I think Rebel was somehow involved as well, but I'm a little fuzzy on the details. It was supposed to be an interview through Facetime a few weeks ago, but then the kid canceled and said he'd contact me later, and now he's here in person. All the better because I much prefer a face-to-face meeting to get a good sense of someone.

Plus, it'll help me take my mind off Joey because I'm spending way too much time thinking about him. Even more after he asked me to teach him about kink. God, the images running through my mind at that request… I can't explain it. He shouldn't be my type, and yet he's all I can picture at my feet, at my hands, at my mercy. I want to hold him, cuddle him, take care of him…

Okay, and maybe hurt him just a little. You know, like a good spanking. I bet his ass would look amazing after it's met my hand. And even more stunning with my cock buried inside him, his ass cheeks all red and glowing. I love fucking a boy right after I've spanked him when he's all clingy and needy and desperate for my touch.

Oh, for fuck's sake. Get a grip.

I feel like a teenager with a crush who can't stop thinking about him. Next thing you know, I'll be asking someone to pass Joey a note in study hall. Sigh. It's rather pathetic and even more because he's straight, but somehow, that doesn't seem to deter my heart. Hopefully, this interview can help me focus on something else.

I study the applicant for a few seconds as he's sitting in the waiting area we created. His foot is tapping on the floor, but I don't think it's out of impatience. It looks more like he can't sit still, like he's in constant motion. The tapping draws my attention to his shoes, which look like Converse, only... bedazzled? They've got sparkling glitter on them, as well as shiny pink and purple stones, unlike any Converse I've ever seen. Maybe a special edition?

My gaze travels up from his feet to the rest of him. He's dang cute—petit, slender, with dark messy hair and the face of an angel. One look at him and my mouth starts to water. God, the viewers will eat him up. And as soon as I'll announce him, Doms will line up out the door for a chance at a scene with this pretty boy.

"Byron?" I say, and he whips his face toward me.

"Yeah. Mr. Tronco, I assume?"

We shake hands. He's so much smaller than me that I actually have to look down to meet his curious brown eyes. "You can call me Hunter. Or Daddy."

His eyes widen. "*Daddy?*"

It sounds weird coming from his lips. Wrong, somehow. I shrug, letting go of his hand. "It's my nickname."

"Oh, okay. For a second I thought you were suggesting you wanted to be my Daddy."

Daddy

I raise an eyebrow. "You have something against Daddy kink?"

I don't say it out loud, but that would be a dealbreaker. If you can't respect other people's kink, you can't work here. No kink-shaming, even if it's something that doesn't turn you on.

"Oh, hell no. Absolutely not. I'm just not interested in a Daddy for me personally."

By all standards, this should disappoint me. Not that I would've ever started something with one of my boys, but dammit, just like Ian, this kid should've hit all my buttons. I've had boys like him. I've loved boys like him. But I can't even muster an ounce of enthusiasm at the thought of being his Daddy—aside from the fact that he shot that down instantly.

"Fair enough. And no, this wasn't a come-on of any kind. I run a respectable business here, Byron, and that means the boys are off-limits for any of my staff. You guys wanna mess around with each other, that's fine. But none of the crew is allowed to touch you, just so we have that clear."

He nods, then bites his lip. "Not the best way to start the interview, is it?"

I smile at him. "You're fine. I don't blame you for being crystal clear on expectations."

"Okay. I'm a little nervous," he says as I gesture for him to take a seat.

"You've never done porn, is that correct?"

He hesitates. "Not voluntarily."

Ah, there's a story there. "What happened, if you don't mind me asking?"

He sighs, and anger flashes in those gorgeous brown eyes. "Someone shot a video of me without my permission and distributed it. Let's leave it at that."

Yeah, he doesn't need to say more. I can fill in the blanks myself. "I'm sorry to hear that," I say, and I mean it.

Look, I love porn, but it's gotta be consensual. Shooting videos of people and uploading them on porn sites without their consent, that's a crime. One that the cops, sadly, don't do all that much about. Too often they assume that since you consented to being filmed in the first place, you had to have known it was gonna be put on the Internet. Yeah, no. Shooting a hot home video to jerk off to together is a whole different ball game than putting it on Pornhub.

"Yeah, it sucked. I lost my job over it, so that's what brings me here. I'm not gonna pretend I have some ulterior motive for being here, some artistic desire to show sex is beautiful or some shit. I need money, plain and simple. Though I will say that I like the idea of reclaiming my body, my autonomy, by shooting porn on my terms, if that makes sense."

I lean back in my chair, folding my hands behind my head. "I appreciate your honesty, Byron. I will say this. In my experience, people who do it purely for the money don't last long. You gotta actually like it."

He grins, and it makes him look adorable. "Oh, don't get me wrong. I love sex. It's not gonna be a hardship to get fucked six ways to Sunday, you know? In fact, I'm kinda looking forward to it. Not to be too personal, but I haven't had a good dicking in forever."

Okay then. "Glad we got that cleared up. So, what kind of experience do you have with kink?"

He pulls one shoulder up in a careless shrug. "Not much, but I'm open to exploring. As I indicated on the application form—and by the way, that form has a major typo as well as a few grammar mistakes that need to be fixed

—the only things I'm not interested in trying are watersports and knife play. Other than that, I'm game."

"Typos and grammar mistakes?"

He waves his right hand dismissively. "I'm a teacher and a grammar Nazi, sorry."

"Feel free to point them out later so I can fix them. But back to our discussion, your hard limits are noted. Did you fill out the soft limits as well?"

"Yeah. I guess I checked off quite a bit, but that's because I'm a total newbie."

I frown. "Byron, are you sure you want to have your first experiences with kink on camera? I can easily get you connected with a club here. That would give you a safe place to do a little exploring on your own."

He looks at me for a bit, then lowers his eyes. "I can't afford to wait. I'm literally one month away from reaching rock bottom in terms of money."

His voice is small as he says those words, and my heart fills with compassion. "Do you have a place to stay? Enough to make rent and buy food?" He peers at me from underneath his lashes as if he wants to gauge how serious I am or what my mood is. "Byron, regardless of whether or not you sign the contract, there's no way I will let you walk out of here unless I know you're okay. I owe that much to Bear and Rebel, though I'm still not entirely sure how you know him. Other than from his videos, that is."

The smile that blooms on his face is beautiful, and I'm happy to see the previous stress disappear. "I met him and Troy when they were on a road trip from LA to Vegas, actually. I got dumped right before an event I was supposed to attend, so Rebel and Troy accompanied me. We had crazy fun."

When he sees my face, he laughs. "Not *that* kind of fun, though not for lack of wanting. Rebel was drunk off his ass, and I take consent seriously. So did Troy, by the way, but even if he had been on board, I wouldn't have done it."

My decision is made. "You're hired."

His face shows pure shock. "Wait...what? Why? I mean, obviously, I'm gonna be awesome at this, but why after I told this story?"

"I did porn, many years ago. I've also owned a BDSM club. If there's one thing I've learned, it's that people assume that when you're a porn star or make your money off sex in any way, you're fair game. They think consent is implied."

"Hell no, it's not. Just because you choose to get fucked by ten guys doesn't mean the eleventh one can just step up and have a go."

I smile at him, strangely proud of the way he said that. "And that's why you're hired. You're good people, kiddo, and we can work out the rest."

He scoffs. "I'm twenty-four, *Daddy*, hardly a kid."

He's right, and while I've always thought of my boys as just that, boys, I've never called them kid or kiddo. Is this part of reaching a certain age? Or is it even more proof—as if I needed it—that my tastes have somehow changed from twentysomething, cute twinks into fortysomething, adorable, and let's not forget *straight* guys? I'm so fucked.

"Let's revisit your preferences. Is there anything you'd like to start with?"

"Whatever you need. As long as we can ease into it."

I nod. "Absolutely. One of the ideas we have is to do series of shoots with progressive kink, so, for example, starting with exploring impact play and gradually building it up, providing both players are fully on board with this."

"Sounds good to me."

And as I look at him, all bubbly and eager to start, an idea starts to form.

11

JOEY

My hands are sweating as I stand outside Kinky Boys Studios, my heart beating wildly and my stomach knotting. I was in some sort of weird trance when I asked him to teach me more about kink. I figured he'd forget about the request afterward, or at least I *hoped* he would. Although part of me also kind of hoped he *wouldn't* forget.

When he texted me last night and told me to swing by the studio so we could talk kink, my stomach clenched so violently I nearly vomited on the spot. Why did he want it to be at the studio? Is he planning to give me a hands-on demonstration? And why does that sound equal parts terrifying and thrilling?

I shuffle my feet, willing them to carry me forward. He's inside, waiting for me, and the last thing I want to do is leave him hanging. Taking a deep breath, I take one step and then another and another until I find myself walking through the door and into the dark, quiet, cavernous space that contains the sound stage.

At first I wonder if I misread his message and got the

wrong day because Hunter doesn't seem to be anywhere. But then I notice something on the bed of the bedroom set that wasn't there before.

If my heart was going wild before, it's absolutely flailing now, my throat going dry as I move closer to look at everything that's laid out, waiting there so seemingly innocently. I've always been vaguely aware that for some people, there's a lot more to sex than inserting tab A into slot B, but I've never given it much thought beyond that. I don't even know what most of the items on the bed are for, although I can make some guesses on a majority of them. Plugs I've definitely seen hundreds of times, but I've generally looked at them as a useful tool. The guys used them to eliminate the need for on-scene prep when it wasn't warranted. But seeing them now, put there by Hunter for the purpose of...of *teaching* me about kink...

To my surprise, my cock starts to harden. Normally it takes a lot of attention to work myself into an erection, well, aside from those random, not-at-all-sex-related erections that pop up at the most inconvenient times.

"Oh good, you're here." Hunter's voice behind me startles me, and I whirl around like I just got busted with my hand in the cookie jar. I wasn't even doing anything but looking, but my face heats anyway.

"Hi, Daddy." The honorific slips off my tongue without thought, and my whole body grows impossibly hotter. "Hunter," I correct myself and clear my throat, moving my hand in front of the half-hard bulge in my jeans in a way I hope looks natural enough not to draw suspicion.

He grins at me, his eyes smoldering. "You know you can call me Daddy."

"I...um..." I stammer. I thought calling someone Daddy was supposed to be *special,* like what Pixie has with Bear.

"It *is* my moniker after all," Hunter tacks on, and I deflate a little.

"Right," I say, forcing an awkward chuckle.

He quirks an eyebrow at me. The teasing leaves his expression and is replaced with concern. "Is everything okay? You seem nervous."

"Nervous?" I laugh again, now sounding even less convincing than before. "No, why would I be?"

He waits a few beats, studying me in a way that makes me itch to squirm under his gaze while also beckoning me to hold still and be good for him. I can honestly say no one has ever made me feel this confused in my life without even trying.

"So." He clears his throat and jerks his head toward the bed. "Since you wanted a bit of 'Kink One-oh-One,' I brought a few visual aids to help go over the basics with you."

I nod, not trusting myself to sound casual anymore. Best to stick to nonverbal responses until my hands stop shaking. I shove them into my pockets and follow his gaze to the items on the bed.

"I'm sure you've gathered by now that kink is extremely varied and individual in a lot of ways. Even two people who practice the same kink might do it in a different way with different needs and goals," he explains, and I nod again, starting to relax a little at his professional and soothing tone. "What I want to go over is by no means the be-all and end-all. This is a brief introduction to some of the kinks I'm planning to have you film in the near future. It's obvious from the first scene you filmed that you like to zero in on the emotions and connection between the men you're capturing on film."

"Yeah," I answer, finally trusting my voice again. Talking

about filming puts me back on solid footing, and something about Hunter's gentle expression tells me he already knew that. "Anyone can point a camera at two people fucking and call it porn, but that's not what I want to do. If you do it right, you can make the viewer *feel* something," I say, emotion spilling from me in a somewhat embarrassing way. "I mean, feel something more than simply aroused," I tack on wryly.

"Yes," he agrees, nodding vehemently. "*That's* why you're the best."

My face warms again, his praise settling in the center of my chest, making me feel like I want to find a way to curl around it and hoard it like a greedy dragon.

"So, teach me how someone is supposed to feel when they're getting hit with that." I jerk my chin toward an intimidating-looking wooden paddle.

"This?" He picks it up.

I watch with curiosity as he grips the handle firmly in one hand and then seems to test it out by smacking the palm of his free hand with a solid slapping sound. My eyes go wide, and I drag my tongue along my bottom lip, unable to pull my gaze off the paddle…or maybe it's his large, strong hands that have me mesmerized.

"Yes," I say in nearly a whisper. "What does *that* feel like?"

"For the Dom or the sub?" he asks, eyeing me with interest. It feels like the question has more layers than I'm able to untangle at the moment.

"For the sub," I manage to answer in spite of my once again rapidly beating heart.

"It feels like surrender. It feels like a deep sense of peace to know your Dom is taking care of you, to know you trust them to only hurt you in the way you need them to."

My body trembles involuntarily, and my cock starts to harden again, pressing against my leg as it thickens.

"Do subs ever come just from that?" I don't even know where the question came from aside from the depraved thoughts suddenly filling my mind—images of being bent over Daddy's thick thighs, naked from the waist down, letting go and trusting him to make me hurt in only the best way.

"If their Dom tells them they're allowed to," he says, a hint of playful danger in the rumble of his voice. I manage to tear my eyes off the paddle and drag them to Daddy's face. There isn't a *hint* of heat in his expression now; it's an entire raging inferno. It feels like I'm teetering on the edge of something treacherous, playing with fire I don't know the first damn thing about.

I take a step back, glancing at the bed and breaking the spell. He sets the paddle back on the bed and picks up the buttplug and a cock ring to talk about edging. I listen, nodding along and doing my best to rein in my body, to bring it back to a place I understand.

DADDY

HE'S GIVING off such mixed signals. I've always prided myself on being able to read people well, subs especially, but Joey is such a hot mess of emotions that I can't make heads or tails of it. All I know is that he's interested, though in what, I can't tell.

One thing is crystal clear. He's a sub. Or at least, he has submissive tendencies. The fact that he asked how it felt for the sub was telling. And god, he's so responsive. He may think he can hide it from me, but he's rock hard. But from what? From what I'm telling and showing him? Or from me?

It can't be me, and yet the signals are getting harder and harder to ignore. There's tension between us, chemistry, and I can't explain that any other way than that he feels the attraction too. But what does that mean? Does that indicate he's not so straight after all? Is he aware of his own feelings, the way he gravitates toward me? The way he leans into my touch every time I put my hands on him, even casually? The way he keeps calling me Daddy in that slightly breathless voice?

All this races through my mind as I explain to him how edging works and how that can be used by a Dom to bring his sub pleasure, though not after frustration and maybe even some pain first. Joey nods, and I move on to tell him something about flogging and impact play in general, letting him hold several types of floggers.

"The good kind of pain brings endorphins, and it can create a rush unlike anything else," I say.

"But not for everyone, right?" Joey checks.

"True. There are plenty of subs who don't like impact play, at least not the kind that involves too much pain. Others totally get off on it. Everyone is different."

Joey swallows visibly. "A-And you? What do you like to do? W-with your boys?"

I smile at him, allowing some of what I feel to shine through on my face. If I wanted to, I could block off every emotion and not let him see anything, but I want him to see that this conversation doesn't leave me unaffected either. If he's even the slightest bit confused, I sure as fuck wanna add to that confusion by giving clear hints where I stand.

"I'm a very hands-on type of Daddy," I say, dropping my voice to a low rumble.

He swallows again. "H-hands-on?"

"Mmm. I use tools like plugs or paddles at times, and I've locked plenty of pretty cocks into cages to make sure my boy behaved, but I really like to use my hands. Take a spanking, for example. It's one of my favorite things to do...and I always use my hands." I hold up my hands, and Joey stares at them, mesmerized. "Trust me, I can pack a wallop in these two."

"Are...are your boys often disobedient that they need a spanking?"

"Sometimes. I'm a very caring Daddy who loves to spoil his boys, but I'm also strict. If I give orders, I expect to be obeyed, and failing to do so results in a punishment."

Joey nods, finally tearing his eyes away from my hands, though he doesn't quite meet my eyes. His cheeks show two red spots, and they look adorable on him. "That seems reasonable," he says, and it takes me a second to understand what he's responding to.

"Does it?"

He shrugs. "If they don't like that, they shouldn't be in a relationship like that. Or a dynamic or whatever it's called because you weren't *together* with all of them, right?"

I'm sure I'm imagining the hint of jealousy in his voice because that would make no sense at all. "True. I've played in clubs with plenty of boys, and those were just scenes." My thoughts go to Lex like they always do when I think about playing in clubs, and I need a moment to breathe before I can continue. "But I've also had boys I was in a relationship with, and I very much prefer the latter."

"So...so you're looking for a new boy now?" Joey asks, the red spots in his cheeks even more prominent.

"Not actively looking because honestly, with starting a

new business, the timing isn't ideal for a new relationship, but if something comes my way, I'd definitely be open to it."

He lets out a sigh. "I was just wondering because you dated Pixie."

I chuckle. "I wouldn't call that dating. We went out for dinner once, and I knew about five minutes in that he wasn't for me. He was Bear's, even if, as you put it, Bear needed some time to pull his head out of his ass."

Joey laughs at that, and it's a good sound, a happy sound. God, I want to make him happy, make him feel good and safe and loved, taken care of. "Bear never stood a chance. Once Pixie has his mind set on something, he's like a little pitbull disguised as a chihuahua. He looks all cute and pretty, but that kid's as stubborn as they come."

I don't know Pixie that well, but that description seems highly accurate from what I can tell. He's got Bear wrapped around his finger—though I think it's mutual.

"Bear is a different kind of Daddy than me. Much more relaxed. Less involved."

Joey frowns. "There's different kinds of Daddies?"

"Oh, for sure. Some Daddies keep the Daddy part to the bedroom, and that's it. Others will get involved in some areas of their boy's lives but not all of it."

"What...what kind of Daddy are you?"

I smile at him. It's a dance we're doing, almost like a handler approaches a skittish horse, a careful back-and-forth where neither of us shows our hand, maybe out of fear of chasing the other one away. Joey has more on his mind than he's willing to admit, but then again, the same is true for me. I'd love to come right out and tell him that I'm fascinated by him, that I want to get to know him better—much better—but I'm afraid that will scare him off. If I'm wrong, if

I'm misinterpreting his messed-up signals, I could lose not only his friendship but my head cameraman as well.

"I'm an all-in Daddy. At least, that's what I prefer."

"So you'd be involved in…"

"…in every aspect of my boy's life. I love making all the decisions except my boy's job and anything that exceeds my privileges as a Daddy."

"Like what?"

"I had a boy once whose mother passed away unexpectedly, and he had to make a decision whether he wanted to sell his childhood home or not. He wanted me to decide for him, but that's outside my purview as a Daddy. I found a good notary for him who could advise him, but other than that, I stayed out of it."

"I can get that. You can't make decisions he could blame you for later. But you'd decide things like…like what to eat? Or what to do?"

"What to wear, what to eat, when to come, how much to spend, what to say no to and what to embrace… I take away all responsibilities and leave only one: obeying Daddy."

The air between us feels charged, electrified, and Joey's wide eyes are trained on mine. It takes seconds before he breaks off eye contact, and when he does, he lets out a sigh that seems to originate in his very soul.

"That sounds nice," he says, his voice barely more than a whisper. "That sounds really nice."

12

JOEY

I've been to plenty of strip clubs, with both men and women getting naked on the stage, and I have to say, I've never understood the excitement. Sometimes the pole work is impressive, I guess. I snort a laugh, hearing Brewer's voice in my head, saying, "that's what he said."

"Are you honestly not getting tired of these big gay outings?" Hunter asks, barely tearing his eyes off the gorgeous man on the stage.

I look at the dancer assessingly. He's good looking. There's no doubt about that. He's dressed in nothing but a black thong, his ass practically a work of art as he shakes it in our direction. His whole body is covered in some kind of glitter that catches the light with every movement, drawing the eye to the contours of his lithe frame.

Without even thinking, I mentally frame the scene, finding the best angle to capture his essence as he moves fluidly. I'm not sure what about this Hunter thinks would upset me. It's a naked man, not exactly front-page news for me.

"I told you. It doesn't bother me."

I shrug and glance at Hunter again. It's difficult to tell in the dim lighting of the strip club if his interest in the man on the stage is purely professional or if it's more. The thought that he might want to bring the boy home and cook him dinner makes me irrationally angry. God knows dinner would be the last thing on his mind if he were to pick someone up to take home, but it's certainly what's on my mind. The idea of Hunter feeding someone else, sitting on the couch and talking for hours, giving them that worried, caring look.

The man turns in our direction and dances closer, a sly smile fixed on Hunter the entire time. "You want a dance, baby?" he asks, slinking closer.

"Actually, I'd like to talk."

The man throws back his head and laughs. "If that's a euphemism, I've officially heard it all."

"It's not a euphemism," Hunter assures him. "I can wait until your shift ends if it's better, though."

He crooks an eyebrow and hops off the stage. "Pay for a dance, and you can talk all you want."

"Fair enough." Hunter reaches into his pocket, pulls out a few folded bills, and hands them over. "I'm Hunter, but most people call me Daddy."

He snorts a laugh and shakes his head, stuffing the money into the waistline of his underwear. "Nice to meet you, *Daddy*. I'm Glam." Glam wastes no time plopping his ass onto Hunter's lap and swiveling his hips. "So, what do you want to talk about? Politics? Religion? Or would you rather I tell you about the shower I took before I came to work tonight. Spoiler alert, it involves a vibrator and a pair of nipple clamps."

For Hunter's part, he keeps his hands to himself, seeming only mildly interested in Glam's teasing, but that doesn't stop my blood from boiling. I clench my jaw and cross my arms to prevent myself from grabbing Glam by the hair and pulling him off Hunter's lap. It makes no sense. Why should I care who touches Hunter? Just because he's made me feel kind of special over the past couple of weeks. It's not like I'm gay. At least I don't think I am.

"None of the above, sorry," Hunter answers with a chuckle. "I'd much rather talk about a job where you could earn twice as much money and only work one day a week."

"Mmm," Glam hums, turning around to face Hunter, straddling his lap and continuing to gyrate his hips. "You want to be my sugar Daddy?"

"Not exactly." Hunter produces a business card, handing it to Glam, who stills for the first time as he reads it.

"Porn?" he says, raising his eyebrows.

"Porn," Hunter confirms.

"I've been hearing rumors that there's a new gay porn studio opening in town, but I wasn't sure I should believe them. You know, I met Rebel from the Ballsy Boys once."

"Small world." Hunter grins. "My studio is actually affiliated with Ballsy, but we're a kinky offshoot."

"Okay, I'm officially intrigued." He shoves Hunter's card into his thong as well. "Tell you what. I'll give you a call to talk more about it tomorrow."

"Sounds good."

"Now, you've got five more minutes left on this dance. You want me to finish, or is your boyfriend going to have an aneurysm?" Glam glances over at me and winks, the corner of his lips quirking in a playful smirk.

"I'm not—" I start.

"No dance," Hunter says, patting Glam's thigh to get him to stand up. "Be sure you call, though."

"Yes, Daddy," Glam purrs.

He hops back up onstage, and I manage to unclench my jaw for the first time.

"Come on, I think we're all set here," Hunter says, standing and tilting his head toward the exit. I follow him out, my blood still pumping loudly in my ears, my gut churning, and my mind racing with confusion.

As we step out of the noisy strip club, the silence of the night is almost deafening. Hunter's steps are slow, as if waiting for me to catch up, but I purposefully walk slower, desperately grappling with my raging emotions. I was jealous of Glam grinding on Hunter, and not just a little jealous. But what the fuck does that even mean? Okay, yeah, I've enjoyed Hunter's attention lately, probably more than I should, but does that mean I'm *into* him?

"Joey?" he says my name gently, and I snap my head up to find him standing only a few inches in front of me. "Tell me what's wrong."

"I—" I cut myself off, shaking my head.

Hunter's expression hardens, and before I know what's happening, he has his hand wrapped around my biceps and leads me toward his car. "Tell me what's wrong," he says again, more sternly this time, caging me in against the passenger side of the car. With anyone else, the move might've made me slightly claustrophobic, but from Hunter, it sends heat racing through my veins.

"I was jealous," I blurt out. "Glam is gorgeous, and he was flirting and grinding on you, and I didn't like it."

His eyebrows shoot up. "It's Glam's job to flirt and grind on people. I paid him nearly a hundred bucks. He was just doing what he thought I wanted him to. Which I didn't, by the way."

I cock my head, not following the convoluted sentence. "You...you *didn't* want him grinding on you?"

"No, not particularly. If I'm being honest, and I'm saying this with full knowledge that it will more than likely bite me in the ass, I haven't been especially interested in anyone recently except for you."

"Me?" I repeat dumbly.

"I know you said you're straight, but—"

Whatever he was about to say gets lost in a muffled sound of surprise as I press my lips to his. It's barely more than a peck, but his hands fall to my hips, gripping them tightly, while his beard scratches against my skin. I pull back almost as quickly as I went in for it. I spin around and yank open the car door, my heart in my throat and my head even more of a mess than it was before.

13
JOEY

Three hours later and my lips are still tingling from the kiss. Can it even be considered a kiss? It was barely a brush of Daddy's lips against mine... *Hunter's* lips. Fuck, I don't even know anymore. Everything inside my head feels like a jumble of confusion and...well, mostly just confusion. Every time I think about the feeling of his mouth on mine, the warmth of his breath on my skin, his sure hands holding on to my hips, deep longing hits me all over again.

It's undeniable that I'm attracted to Hunter, that I want him more than I've wanted anyone before. *That's* not the confusing part. What I can't figure out is how I've gone forty years without realizing I'm gay. Am I even gay? Maybe I'm bi? Or...god, I don't know the whole array of sexual identity options that exist these days.

I bounce my knees, running my hands over my face and trying my damnedest to untangle my thoughts. It would be great to talk to someone who could help me sort this all out, but my closest friend at the moment happens to be Hunter. I suppose I could ask my mom for advice. It's not like she'll remember the conversation afterward anyway.

I mindlessly run my tongue along my bottom lip, and I swear I can still taste Hunter there. My cock hardens at the thought of his smell and flavor lingering on my skin, the intimacy of carrying part of him around with me long after our encounter almost too much to bear.

My phone vibrates in my hand, and I glance down to see Hunter's name displayed. My thumb hovers over the answer icon for several seconds before I hit Decline instead. I'm sure he's calling to check that I'm okay, but I need to figure out the answer to that question myself before I talk to him.

It occurs to me that Hunter may be my only friend in Las Vegas, but he's not my only friend in the world. I could call Bear for advice maybe? I consider that for several seconds and reject it. He's so close with Hunter it wouldn't be fair to put him in the middle of this mess. Then the answer comes to me, and I feel kind of stupid for not thinking of it sooner. Campy spent years actually *doing* gay porn, thinking he was straight the whole time until he met his boyfriend, Jackson. If anyone is able to help me shed some light on this situation, it'll be Campy.

I pull him up in my contacts and hit the Call button before I can think better of it.

"Joey, hey," he answers cheerfully after a few rings.

"Hey," I say back.

"How's Las Vegas treating you? Missing us already?"

I chuckle, some of the tension in my chest easing simply by the sound of his familiar voice. I don't know why I haven't called or texted any of the guys before now. I spent years being close to them. How much I truly miss working at Ballsy hits me full force, adding to the hurricane of emotions already raging inside me.

"Yeah, I miss you guys," I answer. "And Vegas is..." I blow out a long breath, trying to think of how to actually answer that question.

"Want to talk about it?"

"That's actually why I called," I confess.

"Oh? Is everything okay?"

"Yeah, just weird and confusing," I say.

"Weird and confusing are my specialty," he assures me with a laugh. "Hit me with it." I hear a rustling on his end like he's getting comfortable for a long conversation, and my heart warms.

"Did you really have *no* idea you were gay before you fell for Jackson?" I blurt out because honestly, there's no way to start this that wouldn't be awkward.

He barks out a laugh. "Okay, *so* not where I thought this was going, but I can get on board for this. Let's see..." He makes a humming noise like he's thinking, and I wait quietly, holding my breath. "Well, first, I'm not gay. I'm bi. In hindsight, I'd say there were some clues, some crushes I had on other men that I didn't recognize as crushes at the time, that sort of thing."

His answer only makes me more uncertain about my feelings. I can say without a doubt I've never been attracted to a man before. Although...I suppose I've never really wanted a woman the way I was *supposed* to either.

"I see."

I lick my lips again, almost testing myself to see if my reaction is still there, like when you keep pressing on a bruise to see if it still hurts. The same longing crashes into me again at the taste of Hunter lingering on my lips, and I can't decide if I'm relieved or not.

"Is there someone you're attracted to?" Campy prompts.

"Yes, but it's kind of hard to explain."

"Try me," he says.

"Okay, it's like this. On some level, thinking of myself as straight has always been more of a default. When people talk about seeing someone and immediately wanting to fuck them, I can't relate to that at all. Sex is fine, but a big part of me has always felt like I could totally live without it and not have a problem. I've never managed to keep a girlfriend because they always got insecure, thinking I didn't like them because I didn't want to fuck all the time," I explain.

"Hm, okay. But now there is someone you're interested in sexually?"

I take a second to consider his question. At first sex with Hunter wasn't near the forefront of my mind. I craved the attention and care that radiated off him. But now...

"I think so. But what if I'm wrong? What if I *think* I want to have sex with him but end up not being into it?"

"I have a theory about what's going on," Campy says. "Are you the kind of person who will feel better if you have a label, or would you rather I leave that out and I'll just give you advice?"

My heart jumps. He thinks there's an actual label for the way I am? Does that mean there isn't anything wrong with me? That other people feel the way I do?

"Label, please," I answer, nearly choking on the word, my throat feels so tight.

"I think you're on the Ace spectrum," he says.

"Ace, like asexual?" I've heard the term before but never paid much attention to it.

"It fits what you're describing."

"Does that mean I don't like sex at all? Like, if I *did* try to have sex with this person, I definitely won't be into it?" My chest feels like a deflating balloon.

"Not necessarily," he says. "Like all sexuality, it's not

always black and white. A lot of people who identify as demisexual are interested in sex in certain circumstances or when there's an emotional connection."

"How am I supposed to know, then?"

"I think you need to talk to this person, tell them how you're feeling," Campy concludes. "If you're having sexual feelings about them, I'm guessing the two of you are close, right?"

I think back over the past few weeks and how good it felt to get to know Hunter, how he's taken care of me and made me feel safe. "Yeah, we're close."

"Good, then talk to them. Take things slow and see how you feel."

"Okay, yeah," I say, blowing out a breath and rubbing my free hand on my knee.

"And listen, even if you decide you aren't that into sex, that doesn't mean there's anything wrong with you."

"Thanks, Campy, I needed to hear that."

"Anytime," he assures me.

"How'd you know so much about this anyway?" I ask.

"I realized I was so misinformed about bisexuality that after I figured my own shit out, I've dug into other sexualities to understand them all better."

"That's really cool. Do you, um...is there a link with information or anything you could send me?"

"Yeah, of course," he says. "I'll send it as soon as we get off the phone."

"Great, thanks again."

"You're welcome. I'm glad I could help, and good luck with everything."

We sign off, and I set my phone down, feeling a lightness I haven't felt in as long as I can remember. Since the age of thirteen, I've been sure there was something wrong with me.

Knowing that there's a name for how I feel and that there are other people out there feeling the same way is a bigger relief than I ever could've imagined. Campy's right. I need to talk to Hunter about everything, but tonight I'm going to do a little research, using the links Campy just texted me, and tomorrow I'll call Hunter.

14

DADDY

I'll give him one night, but if I haven't heard from him tomorrow morning, I'm heading over to his house. I understand he may need some time to process what happened, even if he initiated it himself. That kiss was everything despite it being brief and relatively chaste. Just his lips on mine for a few seconds at most. But that short time was enough to make my heart race and my head spin.

And it's left me confused as fuck because even though I felt mixed signals, I hadn't seen that kiss coming. Then again, I can't even imagine how messed up *he* must be. He didn't lie to me when he told me he was straight. Or thought he was straight. He legit believed that. And then to find out in your forties that you're not? Yeah, I can allow him some time.

But not too much. Too much time leads to overthinking and worrying. Too much time leads to self-doubt and second-guessing and misinterpreting things in hindsight. So he has until tomorrow morning, and if he doesn't answer my calls then, I'll come see him in person.

I sleep surprisingly well that night. I'd kind of expected

to spend time trying to analyze what happened, look back on all our previous interactions to see what I've possibly missed, but instead, I lay down, thought of that kiss, and fell asleep happy. Let's hope it's a good omen for the conversation that's gonna happen at some point today.

It's Sunday, so no work—though that won't always be the case, since I anticipate doing shootings on Sunday in the future to accommodate people having other jobs as well. But today, we're off. I give Joey till ten in case he wants to sleep in, and then I call him again.

"Hi," he says, picking up almost immediately as if he was waiting for my call, and breathe out with relief.

"Hi. I wanted to check in on you."

He makes a sound like a choked laugh. "I figured you would."

"Yeah? Then why didn't you pick up yesterday?"

There's a rustling noise as if he's making himself comfortable. "I needed some time to process...Daddy."

That last word is added softly, but it hits me like a punch to my gut. If he still calls me that, does that mean that...?

"Talk to me, boy," I say, and that last word flies off my lips as if I've never called him anything else.

"Is that what you'd want me to be? Your boy?" he asks.

He's not beating around the bush, is he? "I'd love to try and see if it's what you really want. If we would be a good fit."

"So you *like* me?"

I smile at the adorable way he worded that. "I've been interested in you for a while, but I didn't want to say anything, since I assumed you were straight."

He exhales slowly. "Yeah, I thought so too." It's followed by a nervous laugh. "Turns out, not so much. I called a friend yesterday—well, Campy, actually, since he knows about this stuff after only figuring out he was bi until he was with Jackson—and he helped me see that maybe I've been thinking about all this all wrong. But it's still confusing and complicated, and I don't know if I have all the right answers and labels yet."

"Boy, I don't give a flying fuck about labels. Just start at the beginning. Talk to me. We can talk through this together."

I'm oh-so tempted to tell him to come over so I can make him breakfast and take care of him, but I think we need this distance now. My self-control is thin, and I don't want to rush into something we may regret later. Joey already means too much to me for that.

"So..." Joey says. "I've never...been with a man. I've been around gay men so much and working in gay porn, but I never once felt attracted to any of them. I guess in hindsight, I liked Bear and Pixie together, but not because I wanted either of them. More because I liked how they were together, their dynamic."

"But you've been with women, correct?"

"Sure, but not a lot, and it never did much for me. I mean, I could get hard, but..."

I have no trouble imagining his face, which is undoubtedly red with that adorable shy look. But he's so brave, talking about this, daring to face this big change in himself.

"...but it never was like you had imagined it would be?" I fill in for him.

"Yeah. I know that most of what I've seen of sex was porn, and porn is different than normal sex between a couple, but it wasn't all fake. And what they showed me was so much more than what I felt. I've seen Tank and Brewer together and Bear and Pixie and that couple we shot the other day, and I've never, ever felt like that during sex. I could see how much they enjoyed it, how much pleasure it brought them. They didn't have to work hard to get aroused or to stay hard… I thought it was because I hadn't met the right woman yet. Turns out…"

It starts to fall into place for me, and I think I know where he's going with this. But it has to come from him. I cannot and will not stick a label on him he's not ready to embrace himself.

"…turns out I hadn't met the right man," he finishes, his voice soft and insecure.

"That's a big thing to admit, sweet boy," I say, the endearment falling from my lips so naturally. "I'm proud of you for having the courage to face this."

"I think I'm demisexual," he blurts out, and then he's quiet.

"Thank you for sharing that with me." I put all the warmth in my voice I can muster. He needs encouragement more than anything else. What a shock this must be to him. "How do you feel about that?"

"Relieved. I thought something was wrong with me, but it's not, is it? It's how I'm wired, and it so happens to be a little different from most folks."

"It is, but it's who you are, and that's never something to be ashamed of."

He lets out another sigh. "But I do feel a little shocked. And stupid. I mean, it's kinda dumb that I never realized I could be attracted to a man until…until you."

"You're calling being attracted to me dumb?" I tease him.

He laughs. "You know I wouldn't. I'm not *that* stupid."

"No, you're not. And I don't like it when you call yourself dumb or stupid, so let's not do that again, hmm?"

He's quiet for a few beats. "I really like it when you say

things like that." His voice has gone soft again, vulnerable with a touch of insecurity. "I like it when you take charge."

In my heart, something stirs. Joy. Excitement. The realization that something beautiful is about to happen. And something soft and warm and cuddly that I can't define. Something with a tenderness that rivals this man's need.

"I love to be in charge," I say equally soft.

"Would you like to be in charge of...of me?"

God, my heart can't hold it, this much sweetness and care. "I would like that very much. Is that what you want, Joey? Do you want to see what it would be like to be my boy?"

"I do...Daddy."

I can't even describe how hearing that word from his lips makes me feel. He puts so much faith in there, so much trust. I can't let him down. And he may not realize it, but he's vulnerable. He's so new to this, practically a baby when it comes to not only kink but being in a relationship as well, let alone a gay relationship.

"I love hearing you call me that," I say. "But, Joey, we'll go slow, okay? In all aspects of this relationship. This is a trial, a test to see if it's what you really want, and you can call it quits at any time."

"Thank you," he says, and the relief in his voice is obvious. "Thank you...Daddy."

15

DADDY

We've agreed to meet later tonight for dinner. I wanted to meet sooner, but Joey said he needed to spend time with his mother, stop by his dad, and do household stuff like laundry and cleaning. He mentioned something about being ashamed if I saw his place right now, so I guess he hasn't prioritized cleaning. No wonder with everything he has on his plate. My hands are itching to step in and relieve him of some of those responsibilities, but I understand we're not there yet.

The hours I have in between give me the opportunity to take care of something I absolutely need to before my relationship with Joey goes any further. I need to talk to Bear. I owe him that much, and so with a heavy heart, I call him.

"Hunter, how are things going?" Bear says as he picks up. I hear someone talking in the background, and Bear says, "Give me one sec."

There's the distinct sound of kissing. "Be careful, baby boy," Bear says. "Text me when you get there, okay?"

Pixie laughs. "I always do, Daddy."

"Yes, you do. You're a good boy for Daddy, aren't you?"

"Good enough to earn a reward?" Pixie says, and I have no trouble imagining the hopeful look on that boy's face. His name is perfectly chosen for him, the little imp.

"We'll talk about that when you get back. Now go, baby boy, or you'll be late."

They kiss again, and even though it's intimate to overhear this, I love being witness to what these two have. It makes me yearn for my own boy even more. For Joey. I want this with him, even if it's not the relationship I thought I would have. I mean, look at Bear. He was adamant about never being with a much younger man, and here he is with Pixie, happier than ever.

"Sorry about that," Bear says to me. "So, how have things been?"

I catch him up on the latest developments for Kinky Boys, and it's clear he's both pleased with and proud of how things are going. It makes the next part even harder. "Bear, there's something I need to tell you."

Bear hmms, then says, "You don't *need* to tell me anything. If this is about what happened in your club..."

"You heard about that?" My stomach drops.

"I don't listen to rumors, you know that."

"What if I tell you the rumors are true?"

He clicks his tongue. "Then I'd call you a liar because the Hunter I know would never be so reckless with someone's life as the rumors make you out to have been."

My eyes well up. It's an emotional feeling to hear someone express so much faith in your character. "At the core, it's true," I say, and then I take a deep breath. "His name was Lex, and he and I had played a few times in my club. He was a little brat, but the fun kind, and he loved earning a punishment. For him, he had to earn it by being disobedient. If I tried to paddle him without that or do a spanking, he couldn't get into it."

"What happened?" Bear asks, his voice is full of concern.

"He filled out all the forms, including the medical waiver and all the limits. Nowhere did he mention he had an existing condition. We did a hard impact scene, and he died of heart failure."

"Oh god..."

"His parents tried to pressure the DA into filing a lawsuit. Apparently, Lex's father is some hotshot lawyer, though in the entertainment industry, so not really the same branch, so to speak. But the DA concluded there was insufficient evidence to prosecute, since he couldn't prove negligence on my part. So the parents started rumors... They went to the press, and I was crucified."

Bear sighs. "Because it looked bad with a gay BSDM club and you as owner doing that scene with a kid who must've been quite a bit younger from what I can tell."

"He was twenty-two. Fresh out of college, about to start in his father's law firm."

"That's way too young to die..."

"I watched him die, Bear. Not sure I'll ever get over that..."

"I can't even imagine. No wonder you needed a fresh start in Las Vegas. I can't blame you for wanting to leave that behind you."

I think about the latest rumors about Lex's parents, then decide those can wait until the moment they turn out to be true. "I doubt it's completely over, but I'm loving Vegas for sure. Which brings me to my next topic."

Bear chuckles. "I knew there had to be a reason why you told me all this now."

Here goes nothing. "You know Joey, your cameraman? Now my cameraman?"

Of course Bear knows Joey. I mentally facepalm myself.

"Is he okay?" Bear asks, clearly concerned.

"Yes, he's fine. He's... Actually, he's come to a sort of discovery you could say, and..."

God, I'm fucking this up. I take a deep breath. "We've started seeing each other. Or we're about to, I should say. We have our first official date tonight."

Finally, it's out. And now we wait.

"You have a date. With Joey. Who used to work for me. Who is straight."

I chuckle. "Bear, my friend, how many times have we discovered that being straight isn't as clear a line as people think it is? Clearly, he's not."

Bear laughs as well. "Touché, though I would've never pegged him for anything else. He never once gave any indication he was into men."

I have no intention of sharing more with Bear than this. That's not up to me. In fact, this is already kind of a borderline case, but I didn't want to go behind the back of one of the few friends I've left.

"It's all very early, but I wanted you to know."

"I appreciate that. You have my... Well, not sure you'd need my permission or my blessing, but whatever. I know you'll treat him well."

"It means a lot to me that you say that, especially after what I told you earlier."

"Hunter, that was not your fault. If the boy didn't share a medical condition he should have, there's no way you could've known. Don't tell me you believe you're in any way responsible."

I sigh. Of course I'm responsible. I should have seen the

signals, the indications. That's what his parents claim as well, that considering the severity of his condition, there had to have been problems before. Symptoms. And I missed them.

"It's certainly made me question myself," I say, and that's as close as I'll get to sharing the depth of the doubt within me.

"I have to admit I'm surprised by the idea of you and Joey, but I do know that you'll take good care of him. You always have with your boys."

Clearly, not good enough, but I keep that part to myself as I vow to do better with Joey.

Joey

I don't have the first clue what Daddy expects of me tonight. He said we can take things slow and see what happens, but what does that *mean*? What if his version of slow is nowhere near my version of slow? And what if I really *don't* want to have sex with him? I know Campy said it was fine if I decide I don't like sex at all, but that's easy for him to say. He isn't in the same predicament.

Whatever interest Daddy has in dating me right now will no doubt evaporate if I don't want to get physical. Maybe I could make it work either way. It's not like sex is torture or anything, and I always managed to make it work with women, even when I wasn't all that excited about it. But something tells me Daddy isn't the type of man who would want an unenthusiastic partner.

He said he'd pick me up and teased me not to wear sweatpants, but that's all the detail he gave about what's in store for me. Will this be a simple dinner date? And if so, what makes it different than the dozens of times we've had dinner together since I started working for him?

I smooth my hands over the front of my shirt, hoping I'm dressed well enough for wherever we're going. I pull out my phone and check the time, then fiddle with a few random apps to kill a few minutes and take my mind off the excruciating wait.

"You didn't have to stand down here. I would've come up to the door like a proper gentleman," Daddy says, his voice that deep rumble that has managed to seep into my bones.

I glance up, fumbling to shove my phone into my pocket at the same time. "You didn't say, so I wasn't sure what I was supposed to do..." I bite down on my bottom lip. I've generally been a confident man, sure of myself in my work and not a total mess in my meager personal life, but there's something about Daddy that makes me feel unsteady. I want to be exactly right for him, but I don't have any idea how.

"That was my mistake. I should've been more clear with my expectations. I'm sorry," he says, stopping right in front of me. "I'll be honest. I've never dated someone so new to the lifestyle. I've always played with more experienced subs," he explains, and I feel myself wilt. Of course I'm messing this up already. I don't know what a sub is supposed to be like, aside from pretty and perfect. I'm not sure if I can pull off those big doe eyes and breathy sighs that seem to come so naturally to the other subs I've met.

"Joey," he says my name firmly, putting a hand under my chin and tilting my face up so I'm looking directly into his eyes. "I didn't mean that there's anything lacking with you. I meant that *I* keep second-guessing myself. I'm afraid to push too hard or come on too strong and scare you away.

Normally I wouldn't have hesitated to tell you *exactly* what I wanted you to do to prepare for our first date, including what you should wear and where you should wait for me. But I wasn't sure if you were ready for that."

I swallow hard, my throat feeling entirely too tight all of a sudden.

"I want that," I admit in a quiet voice. "Treat me like I'm yours." I have no idea where those words come from, but they feel so right on my lips I don't even consider trying to backtrack. This whole situation is weird as hell, but in for a penny, in for a pound.

Daddy's eyes darken with the heat I've started to love seeing there. The look warms me up inside too and makes my nerve endings dance. He cups my jaw, holding my face in place.

He nods resolutely. "Next time, wait for me to come to the door like a good boy."

Next time? He's already sure there will be a next time? My stomach swoops, and my lips tilt in an uncertain smile. "Yes, Daddy," I answer because it feels right, not just because it's what everyone else calls him.

He leans forward and brushes his lips over mine. Like last time, it's hardly more than a whisper of a kiss, but I feel it all the way down to my toes. I sway forward, gripping the front of his shirt for balance as his arms come around my waist, drawing me in and protecting me in one simple movement.

The kiss is over before I know it, but Daddy holds me in his arms a minute longer, letting me feel the rapid beating of his heart under my palm and the solid strength of his body.

When he lets me go, I only have a momentary flicker of disappointment before he grabs my hand, even though we're only three steps from his car. He opens the car door for me like he always does, and once I slide inside, he leans in and fits my seat belt around me, clicking it into place just like I imagined he would over a month ago. He brushes a kiss to my cheek, his beard tickling my skin.

He *does* take me to dinner, and it's not so different from the other meals we've shared recently. Except when he orders for me this time, it feels different, even better than when he's done it before. I'm not sure how to act, so I take my cues from him, treating it like any other time we've hung out—making casual conversation and generally enjoying his company.

Once we're finished with our meal, my nerves have evaporated, replaced by the firm certainty that no matter what else happens, Hunter has become my closest friend and someone I know I can trust.

When he leads me back out to the car, I'm disappointed that the night is ending so soon, but I can't think of a way to ask to go home with him that won't make it sound like I'm ready for more than I actually am. Not that I'm some shrinking flower or innocent virgin, but the sooner we jump into bed, the sooner I might find out that this isn't going to work out, and I'm not ready to stop hoping for it just yet.

"Thank you for dinner. It was really nice," I say when he slides into the driver's seat after helping me in and buckling me again just like he did when he picked me up.

"The night isn't over yet unless you want it to be."

"Oh? What else do you have planned?" I ask, lighting up.

"Do you like chocolate?" he asks with a grin.

"Who doesn't like chocolate?"

It turns out part two of the date is a tour of a chocolate factory, complete with lots of free samples. After the tour, we head into the attached botanical cactus garden, illuminated with Christmas lights on the cactuses to light the path.

Daddy takes my hand, and I get lost in how large and warm and strong it feels wrapped around mine. I lean into him as we stroll, tilting my head back in hopes of catching a glimpse of some stars overhead. No such luck, thanks to all the light pollution, unfortunately.

He catches the gesture and gives my hand a squeeze. "On our next date, we can drive out into the desert and find a nice dark spot to look up at the stars."

"Yeah? You'd want to do that?" I don't just mean looking at the stars, but I can't bring myself to come right out and ask if he honestly wants a second date with me.

"Of course. That sounds really wonderful, actually. Living in New York and now moving here, I can't remember the last time I had the chance to properly look at the night sky. It sounds peaceful."

"Yeah," I agree, trying to think back to the last time I had. It's probably been more than a decade. "Why'd you move here?" I asked before, and it was obviously a sore subject, but it feels important. It feels like something I should know if we're going to see where things might go. Then I see Daddy's eyes change, and the pain and sorrow on his face make me regret that question instantly.

16

DADDY

Of course I knew it would come up at some point. It's not like I'd planned to keep this from him. On the contrary, I've always been a huge advocate for clear and open communication. It's crucial in general but even more so when you engage in kink. If you don't communicate with each other when you do scenes, things can go horribly wrong. I've lived the most horrific consequences of a failure in communication you could imagine.

I'd just hoped it wouldn't come up this soon. And selfishly, maybe I wanted to have a little more time with Joey before having to get this serious. We had such a lovely evening, getting to know each other, enjoying each other's company, and now strolling through this beautiful garden. It's everything I could've hoped for, so wonderfully romantic. And now he looks devastated, and I feel the same way, since I know this is not going to be an easy conversation.

"Forget I asked," Joey says softly. "It's clear this is not a topic you want to talk about."

I lift our joint hands and press a tender kiss on his. "Let's sit down for a bit." I point toward an iron bench, and he allows me to gently pull him over there. "You shouldn't be sorry that you asked. It's a normal question, and you couldn't have known it would be a hard conversation for me. But as you've guessed, this is not an easy story for me to share."

"It's okay if you don't want to talk about it," Joey says, but I shake my head.

"No, though I appreciate you saying that. I don't want to keep secrets from you, and you have every right to know. Just give me a second while I think about the best way to begin."

Telling Bear what happened was easier. Even if he'd been upset with me or had blamed me, it only would've cost me a friendship. A valuable friendship and I won't deny it would've hurt deeply, and it would've had a lot of practical repercussions, what with working with him and all, but this is different. With Joey, there's so much more at stake. It makes me realize how quickly my feelings for him have developed far beyond a simple crush.

"I owned a club in New York, Balls to the Walls. It was a gay BDSM club where we catered to audiences from all over the country. We were known for having strict admission standards, thorough vetting, and the best safety and security procedures you could possibly think of. For ten years, I built the club's reputation and my own with it, and I loved it. I was the owner, but I also played. With my own boys if I had one, or I did scenes with whoever was available in the club."

"Just Daddy care scenes?" Joey asks. "Or did you do more than that?"

"The focus was on Daddy care, but I also did mild BDSM scenes. Over the years, my preferences have definitely grown far more toward the gentler side of Daddy care, but I started out as an all-round trained Dom, so I have experience in a lot of aspects. Lex was new to the club. We ran a background check on him, like we did with everyone, and nothing specific came up. No prior records, no warning signs, nothing. So we admitted him as a rookie member, which is what we call our first-year members. It means they have limited options within the club and are more supervised than our senior members. We just want to make sure they know what they're doing before we allow them to roam free, so to speak."

I take a deep breath as I picture Lex, still so vivid in my mind. "He was beautiful, Lex. Tall, slender to the point of being too thin, pale skin with freckles, a gorgeous boy. He was a little brat, often goading Doms into punishing him. It's what he needed, what he wanted. Like all new members, he had filled out a ton of forms. And this is not a formality. Someone from the club, either me or one of my two managers, would go through every single item on the application form. Hard limits, soft limits, any previous traumatic experiences we needed to know about, any known triggers... and any medical issues. I did the intake with Lex myself, and his form was standard. Nothing specific, nothing stood out... no medical issues. He was twenty-one when he joined, which is young but clearly of age. He had signed off on the medical release form, stating that he had no known prior conditions that were in any way relevant to his activities in the club."

I can tell Joey senses where this is heading because the pressure on my hand increases slightly. It's a comfort, and I'm grateful that he allows me to tell the story without wanting me to jump to the conclusion.

"The medical part, we can't check. We're not allowed to pull records from doctors or something, you know? So we have to trust that members tell us the truth, and in those ten years, I've never had an issue. Until Lex. We'd done four scenes together, but he'd also done a few scenes with some of the other Doms. Afterward, I checked with all of them, and none of us noticed anything out of the ordinary. He didn't use his safeword, he didn't give any indication he was unwell, and his body never showed any sign it was getting too much. Until that last scene."

My voice breaks on those last words, and I take the time for a few calming breaths before I continue.

"He loved the paddle, and I'd promised him we'd push his limits a little further that day. I'd gone over the safeword procedure with him, double-checked before we started he was still okay with it. Everything seemed fine until he passed out on my lap. At least, I thought he'd passed out. When his body went slack, I stopped immediately, of course, and then we discovered he had no heartbeat. We tried to resuscitate him, used the AED we had in the club, but it was too late."

Joey gasps, his grip on my hand painfully tight. "How is that possible? He was young, right?" Then it hit him, what I said about the medical issues. "He had some kind of disease, didn't he?"

I nod slowly, still fighting to keep my composure. "Yes. He had a heart condition, which caused his heart to pump badly, which in turn affected his whole body, including his lungs. He was on medication, and he was on the transplant list for a new heart. I found all this out afterward, though. But he never told us. He never told me. He signed off on having no medical issues, and we believed him. Sure, in hindsight, there were certain indications. How pale he was, the fact that he seemed to be out of breath quickly, him being so thin and frail. But he was fair-skinned, you know?

You don't look for something if you don't know you should."

"God, I can't even imagine how you must have felt," Joey says softly. "For someone like you, who is always so focused on taking care of your boys, that must've been a devastating blow."

My chest fills with breaths of relief, even as my eyes get a little misty at hearing those sweet words. "It was. I was furious with him for not telling us the truth, but I was also furious with myself for not seeing it."

"So, what happened? Did you close the club?"

"I sold it. The guys who own it now were my two managers, who worked there for years, so I know they'll do a great job running it."

Joey looks at me with a slightly puzzled expression. "So did you leave out of guilt? Or because being in the club reminded you of what had happened?"

Here comes the hardest part, the part that still fills me with shame every time I think about it. Shame and anger.

"Lex's parents didn't believe it was an accident. In their defense, though they knew Lex was gay, they had no idea he was active in the BDSM scene. He'd never told them, knowing they would try to stop him from going, just like he'd never told us about his condition. His parents went to the cops, then to the district attorney's office, trying to persuade the DA to bring charges against me. The DA subpoenaed all records, which I handed over gladly. All the forms he'd signed and filled out, video footage of some of his previous scenes, and the footage of his last scene."

"You film everything in your club? That seems like a breach of privacy," Joey says.

"We film for exactly this reason. It's a closed circuit while the scene is going on, so someone can monitor at all times.

That's necessary because we have some closed rooms that can't be monitored any other way, since they have no windows. But that footage is never shown to anyone, except in circumstances like this. We store all videos for six months, and then they're automatically deleted and overwritten with newer ones. That's why we didn't have the first few scenes Lex did on video, but we had the last six months. Eight scenes in total, including three with me."

"Okay, that makes sense. But the papers and the footage must've shown it wasn't your fault. Right?"

I nod. "In the end, it did, but the DA wasn't happy about it. Look, we're an easy target, you know? A gay BDSM club, that's so far outside of what most people consider normal that it's not hard to paint it in a bad light. And trust me, the DA *wanted* to come after us. The problem for him was that I'd covered my ass. I had proof that Lex hadn't informed us. His parents tried to convince the DA that we'd forged the documents, that they were fake, and that we had hidden the real ones, so the DA had handwriting analysis done by various experts. They compared the forms we had with other examples of Lex's handwriting, and of course, it was completely identical. That, plus the footage of all the previous scenes, was enough proof for the DA that even though he didn't like it, he had no legal grounds to press charges. So he dropped the case."

"That's good news, right? So I may be missing something, but I still don't really understand why you wanted to move. Was that because of the memories?"

"Partly. I'll admit that stepping back into the club after Lex's death was incredibly hard for me. But what was even harder was that even within my own community, a lot of people believed I was guilty. Not so much of killing Lex directly but of negligence. This was thanks to a big campaign Lex's parents started by spreading rumors about me within the gay community. My reputation was in tatters, and even though those closest to me, like my two managers at the time, believed me, the damage was done. Attendance in the club dropped rapidly, and we were losing members fast. I didn't want to bring down the club with me, so I decided to sell it and leave."

Silence hangs in the air, but it's not a heavy silence. It feels comfortable, and I'm so relieved I've told Joey the truth. Whatever happens now, at least he knows the real reason I'm here, which means he can decide for himself what to do with that information.

"I'm so sorry," Joey says with a lot of warmth in his voice. "I'm sorry for that poor kid who died way too young, and I'm sorry that his parents lost him at such a young age, but I'm also sorry for you. This wasn't your fault, you know that, right?"

I smile because he sounds exactly like Bear. "Rationally, I know that, but emotionally, it's been hard to let go of feelings of guilt. I blame myself for not paying more attention, for missing signs. In hindsight, there—"

"There's a reason why the saying goes, hindsight is always 20/20," Joey interrupts me. "Of course it's easy in hindsight to see signals. But that's because you now know what to look for. You said it yourself, everything you noticed had a logical explanation other than the rather unlogical explanation, which was that he had a serious condition he'd kept hidden from you. How could you have possibly known to expect that? I mean, he knew he had this condition. He deliberately hid it, so in a way, this is his own fault, isn't it? I know that sounds harsh, but it's the truth."

He's not the first person to say it. Marcus and Casey, my two former managers, told me the exact same thing, but hearing it from Joey means everything. It's like the wound that's been bleeding inside me ever since that horrible day is closing a little.

"Thank you," I say, and I pull him close, wrapping my arm around him.

And when he hesitates briefly but then puts his head on my shoulder despite everything that happened, I feel like the luckiest man on the planet.

We sit for a bit like that, and then I lean back, searching Joey's face. "I would very much like to kiss you, but it's okay if you're not ready for that."

"I am," he says quickly. "I mean, I would like that. For you to kiss me...Daddy."

God, I love the way that word falls from his lips, so breathy and thoughtful. Never a mindless habit but always with care. "My sweet boy," I whisper against his lips, and then I bring our mouths together.

The first touch is soft but electric, his lips hesitant against mine. I take my time with him, licking his lips, wetting them until he opens up and lets me in. He tastes so sweet, his tongue moving against mine, carefully exploring and seeking. I allow him to take the lead, not wanting to come on too strong. He needs to set the pace here.

He wraps his arms around me and holds on tight, and I do the same, pressing our bodies together. This is perfect. He is perfect.

By the time he breaks off the kiss, he's panting, his lips glistening and swollen. I gently wipe them off with my thumb. "That okay?"

"That was..." He sighs, but it's a happy one. "That was more than okay."

"I know," I say, kissing him one last time. "It was perfect."

17

JOEY

Daddy: Put on that pair of jeans that makes your ass look fantastic and your black T-shirt. I'm picking you up for another hunting trip.
Joey: A hunting trip?
Daddy: We're still short one Kinky Boy
Joey: Ah, that kind of hunting trip, haha. I'll get dressed now and wait for you.
Daddy: Good boy

EVEN JUST READING the words on the screen, I swear I can hear the deep growl of Daddy's voice washing over me with the praise. Also, I absolutely love it that he tells me what I should wear. There's no guesswork this way, no potential to show up and feel embarrassed that I'm over- or under-dressed.

If there was any question about whether I'd like being in the submissive role in a relationship, that's long gone. True to his word, we've taken things slow. Like snail-pace slow. He's taken me on numerous dates now, but we have yet to get past the kissing stage. The thought of going further makes me nervous as much as it excites me, but I think I'm ready to try.

I set down my phone and change into the clothes Daddy told me to wear. Just putting them on gives me a warm thrill in my stomach, knowing he'll be pleased to see I did as he asked. It may sound strange, but him telling me which clothes to wear makes the ordinary clothes feel like an embrace directly from him.

There's a knock at my apartment door a few minutes later, just as I'm slipping my shoes on. I pull the door open and immediately step into his arms. I've always been a toucher and a hugger, but Daddy brings it out in me even more. I can't think of a better feeling in the world than his arms wrapped around me.

"Hi, sweet boy," he greets me, circling one arm around my waist and using the other hand to tilt my chin so he can press his lips to mine. The kiss is hot and sweet all at once as his tongue pushes into my mouth like he owns me. He holds me so tightly I couldn't get away if I wanted to, and there's no way in hell I want to. I kiss him back, following his lead, hot sparks of arousal bursting inside me as I give in to the feeling of surrender.

Daddy moves his hand off my chin and grabs my ass. I gasp into his mouth as his hand kneads my ass cheek through my jeans, and my cock grows hard, pressed against him.

"I want you to touch me, Daddy," I moan against his mouth, grinding my erection against him, my eyes rolling back as he grabs my ass harder. I still don't know how I'll feel when we actually do get naked together, but this is already so much different than it's been with anyone else.

A groan rumbles in his chest. "If you're telling me you're

ready, then you can bet your ass I'm going to touch you. But it's going to have to wait until a little later."

"Why?" I whine. Later I might not be this excited. What if this is our only chance?

He stops kneading me and gives my ass cheek a startlingly quick smack. A jolt of surprise goes through me, my cock growing even harder. I groan, sagging against him and pushing my ass out.

"Do that again," I beg breathlessly. I want to see if it'll feel as good if I'm expecting it. I want to undo my pants and shove them down to see what it will feel like against my bare skin instead of being dulled by the denim of my jeans.

"No," he says, kissing my forehead and taking a step back. I whimper in protest, and Daddy chuckles. "The first time I lay you over my lap and spank your ass red I'm going to take my time. Right now, we have an Uber driver waiting outside for us."

"An Uber driver?" I repeat, trying not to focus too much on the "spank your ass red" part, because if I do, I know I'll embarrass myself with shameless pleading.

"My car was making a weird sound, so I had to drop it off at the shop to get looked at," he explains. "Now come on, be a good boy, and we can go back to my place after this," he bargains. My heart flutters at the offer. I've been to his apartment plenty of times, but does it mean something more now that we're dating? I mean, of course it does, but what are his expectations?

"Stop worrying so much," he says, clearly seeing the wheels in my head turning. "Be good and trust Daddy."

"Yes, Daddy," I promise, doing as he says and letting my worries fade away. I *do* trust him, so this is an easy command to obey.

"Good." He takes my hand and leads me outside.

The Uber driver seems unconcerned with our long absence, scrolling through his phone until we slide into the back seat of the car. The first thing I notice once I'm seated is a ceramic mug taped to the center console, facing the back seat. The mug has a rainbow flag on the front and a Post-it note affixed to the front that says Tip a Bitch.

I cast a glance at Daddy, who offers me a wry smile in return.

"So, headed to the gay bar tonight?" the driver asks as he pulls out onto the street. He doesn't pause to let us respond before going on. "You look like the kind of man with an impressive job. What do you do for a living?" I have no doubt he's talking to Daddy because I'm positive I look like a forty-year-old man who is barely holding his shit together.

I see a few seconds of hesitation on Daddy's face before his eyes flick to the mug, and he smiles. "I own a gay porn studio."

"Shut the front door," the driver squeals. Thank god we're stopped at a red light because he whips his body around to gape at us for a few seconds. "You seriously make porn? What studio? Oh, my fucking god, this is the best night ever."

I bite the inside of my cheek to keep from laughing, and I get the feeling Daddy is doing the same thing. "The light's green," he points out.

"Oh, fuck me," the driver mutters, turning to face the road again.

"To answer your question, it's a new studio, I'm still getting it off the ground," he explains.

"Are you still hiring because I know the *perfect* guy." He grabs his phone, not seeming to have any concerns about whether or not it's safe to look through Instagram while he's driving because he instantly opens it and starts to scroll.

"Okay, so this guy Max, he works at Vipers. It's a gay bar in town, and I swear to god he has a twelve-inch dick."

"Really?" Daddy's voice holds interest as he sits forward. "Give me that, please, and pay attention to the road so we don't crash," he instructs, taking the phone to get a better look at the picture he's pulled up.

"I haven't actually seen his dick," the driver admits. "But *everyone* says it's twelve inches, hand to god."

"Do you know him personally?" Daddy asks.

"Oh yeah, he's my best friend."

Daddy quirks an eyebrow in my direction, wordlessly questioning the "best friend" part of the story. No one sounds this excited about a friend's dick. Just saying.

"Do you think he'd be open to talking to me?"

"Oh, one hundred percent." He nods like a bobblehead, turning to look back at us again.

"Eyes on the road," Daddy chides for a second time. "And take us to Vipers instead, please."

"You got it."

Daddy

I'm glad when our Uber driver—his name is Benton, according to the Uber app—parks in front of a building with a huge neon sign that says *Vipers*. And in this case, it's only partially because I'm excited to meet the guy with the twelve-inch cock. Benton is a character for sure, but my hands are a tad clammy after the way he drove.

"This is it," Benton announces. "Max is working, so you'll find him behind the bar. Tall guy, a lovely ginger, built like a bear. You can't miss him."

I suppress another laugh because seriously, this guy cracks me up. Joey's eyes are sparkling as well.

"Thank you for the tip, Benton." I drop twenty bucks in his tip jar, knowing this will be preferable to him to tipping through the app.

"You're welcome, boss." Benton turns half around and hands me a business card. "This is me. Call me if you ever need a driver for anything. It can be through Uber, but I also hire myself out as a private chauffeur. Whatever you need."

With a smile, I tuck his business card into my wallet. "Thanks. I will definitely keep that in mind."

"Have fun, and tell Max I said hi!" Benton calls out when we exit the car.

He drives off with screeching tires, and Joey and I burst out laughing. "Oh my God, that's the most insane Uber driver I've ever had in my life," Joey says. "I wasn't sure whether to laugh or to pray that we would arrive safely."

"Amen to that," I say. "And trust me, I *was* praying."

Vipers looks like every bar I've ever been to, though it's clearly aimed at the gay clientele. The neon sign is flashy, and when we open the door, we're greeted by a cacophony of voices mixed in with a song from the Pet Shop Boys. Either it's eighties night, or the owner really loves old-school music. Not that I'm complaining, mind you. I've always kept an affinity for the music I grew up with.

Joey slips his hand into mine as we walk into the bar, and it gives me a warm feeling in my stomach. On some level, I'm still amazed at how okay he is with all this. For someone who didn't know he was gay or maybe bi—I'm not sure he's figured that part out entirely yet—he's certainly okay with it all. Then again, I guess that was to be expected, considering he's been around gay men for the last ten years. It's not like he hasn't had good role models in that sense.

"That has to be Max," Joey says, discreetly pointing at the tall redhead behind the bar. He's exactly as Benson described him, though he forgot to mention the guy is hot as fuck. Maybe he was right that they are just best friends, though I've never talked about my best friend's dick like that. Clearly, I've been missing out, or maybe it's a generational thing.

"Let's sit at the bar," I suggest, and we take two seats at the bar, which has been polished until the shine is almost blinding.

It doesn't take Max long to spot us, and when he walks over, he has a polite smile on his face. "Hi, guys, what can I get you?"

If we'll be playing later, no matter how limited it will be, that means no alcohol. I've always been strict about that, and even though Joey is much older than the boys I've been with so far, that's no reason to change that rule.

"Club soda with lime for me and a Coke for him," I order.

"Coming right up," Max says.

Joey looks at me quizzically. "No alcohol when we intend to do something later," I explain, keeping it vague on purpose. "Consent means you have to be sober enough to give consent, and I'd like to err on the side of caution, especially since it will be our first time."

Joey nods in understanding, and I am astonished all over again at how easily he accepts my decisions for him.

Max returns quickly with our drinks, and when he puts them in front of us, I say, "Benton said to tell you hi from him. He was our Uber driver over here."

Max's face breaks out in a wide smile, and this time, it's a real smile, not the professional friendliness he displayed earlier. "Well, you're still alive, so that's a good sign," Max jokes.

"Barely," Joey quips.

That makes Max laugh even more. "You know, he's never had an accident. I'm telling you, he has to have a triple number of guardian angels assigned to him or something because it's a fucking miracle he hasn't hit anyone yet."

I raise my eyebrows in surprise. "Yeah, that is surprising to hear. I have to say, though, that his reviews on Uber are amazing. He has, like, a four point nine average, and he's done thousands of trips."

Max's eyes soften. "That always amazes me as well. You'd think that with how extravagantly gay he is, he would have at least a few homophobic remarks, but he has only, like, two or so. He's just so likable and genuinely kind that it's almost impossible for people to hate him."

The way Max talks about his friend not only is a sure sign of their good, solid friendship but also indicates the kind of person he is.

"Benton also had some nice words about you," I say, dropping my voice a little lower. The two barstools next to us are empty, but I have no intention of embarrassing Max.

Max looks intrigued, and he leans forward with his arms resting on the bar. "Did he, now?"

I lift a business card out of my wallet and hand it to him. It doesn't take him long to scan it, and I can see the exact moment it hits him because his eyes go wide.

"What exactly did Benton say about me?" he asks.

I smile at him. "Apparently, you're rather *well endowed*."

Max's cheeks flush fiery red. "Oh. My. God. I'm gonna fucking kill him." He groans, burying his face in his hands for a few seconds, shaking his head. "I cannot believe he told you that. Why the fuck would he tell that to complete strangers?"

"In his defense, it was after I told him I own a porn studio. We were on our way to a gay club, scouting potential new boys, and he suggested we'd come here to talk to you."

Max drops his hands and faces me again, his cheeks slightly less red. "I should've known. That guy has never met a stranger in his life. Plus, the whole concept of privacy and too much information is completely foreign to him."

I give him a little while to collect his thoughts because he's been clearly blindsided. But then I ask, "Aside from your understandable embarrassment, is this something you'd even be remotely interested in? And please know that *no* is a perfectly acceptable answer. I will respect that, and we'll just sit here, have a drink, and hang out."

Max studies me, his eyes slightly narrowing, and I keep eye contact with him. "Are you legit?" he asks. "This is Vegas, man. You have no idea how many scammers this city attracts. And no offense, but I can tell from your accent you are not from around here. New York, right?"

People always underestimate bartenders, but the good ones are smart and perceptive, and Max proves that. "Yeah, I'm from New York City. Born and raised in Brooklyn. And yes, I am for real. Have you ever heard of the Ballsy Boys Studio?"

Max rolls his eyes at me. "Dude, what gay man hasn't? You'd have to have lived under a rock for the last ten years."

I point at Joey. "This is Joey, their former head cameraman, who is now working for me. My studio is officially partnered with Ballsy Boys, and Bear, the owner, and I are good friends. You can contact him for a reference if you want."

Max extends his hand to Joey. "Nice to meet you. I have

to say I really admire your work. There's a huge gap between the quality of Ballsy Boys and everyone else."

Joey shakes his hand. "Thank you. I appreciate you saying that, and I couldn't agree more. It's what we aim for with Kinky Boys as well, that same level of quality in the actors, the scenes we set up, and the way we shoot them."

Max nods slowly, then turns his attention back to me. "And you're interested in me only because of the size of my *equipment*?"

"Hell, yes. Do you have any idea how popular big dicks are in porn?"

Max's mouth pulls up in a cheeky grin. "Not just in porn..."

I chuckle. "Yeah, I bet you have no trouble finding willing partners. Look, I'm not gonna lie to you. If your *equipment* had been the only thing you had going for you, I might not have approached you. Not everyone is suitable for the camera, you know? That doesn't mean we're looking for perfect men. Six-packs are not a requirement. In fact, we're striving for a variety of body types, and you would fit in very well."

Max holds my gaze for a few seconds, then lets out a slow breath. "I'll need to think about this. Unlike Benton, I don't do things impulsively. Well, aside from hookups, but that's a different ballgame. Worst-case scenario, you get a clingy guy or someone who's clearly better at bragging than at performing, in which case you walk away. But if I do this, it will have more consequences if it doesn't work out, you know?"

"Completely understandable, so take your time and let me know. I wouldn't want you to do this on impulse, because as you said, this is a decision that can have consequences for you, your life, and your family and friendships as well."

Max grins suddenly. "Benton would fucking love it. He would get such a kick out of this."

I love the way those two talk about each other. It's clear how much affection they have. "Well, I've heard stranger reasons to go into porn than to make someone else happy. Anyway, let me know when you've made a decision. For now, what do I owe you for the drinks?"

He straightens himself. "Nothing. Men who proposition me for porn get their drinks for free."

He winks at me before he steps away and attends to other customers.

All in all, I think that went much better than I'd expected. I'm excited that I'm finally making headway in finding the right boys to contract. Now that this is done, it's time for the next item on today's agenda.

I turn toward Joey. "The sooner you finish your Coke, the sooner we can go home and proceed with the more *entertaining* part of this evening."

I've never seen a man down a drink so fast.

18

JOEY

After our exceptionally colorful Uber driver on our way *to* the bar, it's a little disappointing to get a boring guy on the way *from* the bar to Daddy's place. Although considering how anxious I start to get once we're on our way, it's probably for the best that he just drives and keeps his eyes on the road the whole time.

I follow Daddy up to his apartment, discreetly wiping my sweaty hands on my jeans as we make our way up the stairs to the second floor. As turned on as I was kissing him before, I still don't know exactly how I'll feel if we get naked or if he touches me. I'm positive I want that spanking he teased me with, but what if that's *all* I want? Will he be let down? Will he be angry?

As much as I want to think he'll understand if that's the way things go, I've seen how upset partners in the past have gotten when I put a pause on things before the main event, so to speak.

He unlocks the door and holds it open so I can step inside. I don't look at him while I take off my shoes, my stomach fluttering with nerves. Daddy doesn't say anything as he takes off his own shoes and then grabs my hand again and leads me to the living room. He eases down onto the couch and tugs me onto his lap, putting his arms around me.

"Something that the BDSM lifestyle encourages that vanilla relationships often struggle with is open communication about physical relationships," he says.

I nod slowly. He's right. Every relationship I've been in, most things have just been *expected* without any conversation about them.

"So, you're going to tell me what you want?" I ask, swallowing around the lump forming in my throat. What if I can't give him what he wants?

"No, sweet boy." Daddy shakes his head. "You're going to tell *me* what *you* expect, and then, because I'm your Daddy, I'm going to take care of you."

"Oh." The word falls from my lips on a breath. Can it really be that simple? "What if it isn't what you want? What if it isn't enough?"

"Do you know why being a Daddy has always appealed to me?" he asks, and I shake my head. "It's because nothing gets me hotter than knowing I'm giving my boy *exactly* what he needs." His words are a deep rumble, rolling over my skin and giving me goose bumps, like the first distant echo of thunder before a summer storm comes on.

"I want you to spank me."

A slow smile creeps over Daddy's lips. "I thought you might. What else do you want?"

"I'm not sure," I admit, running my tongue over my bottom lip anxiously. "I want to feel your hands on me, everywhere."

Daddy drags his nose against the curve of my jaw, his

breath fanning along my skin. "I can do that. Is that all for tonight?"

"I think so. But hopefully more later?"

"We'll worry about later when it comes," he assures me. "For now, there are a few more things to go over before we can play."

I nod, relaxing against him, my nerves settling at the calm authority in his tone. He knows what I want and what I'm not ready for, and he doesn't sound disappointed at all. If anything, the heat in his eyes is burning more strongly than ever.

I can feel his cock against the curve of my ass, half-hard and *big*. His arousal makes my cock come to life. It thickens in the confines of my jeans as he runs a soothing hand up and down my back while we talk. It strikes me how intimate this moment is, how much trust I'm putting in him, and that thought only turns me on more.

"First, I need to know if you have any medical conditions that you're aware of?" The weight of the question is obvious in his eyes, and I reach over and run my fingers through his beard in a calming motion.

"No. No medical conditions," I answer.

"Okay, then the next thing we need is a safeword. If at any point you aren't feeling comfortable, all you have to do is use your safeword, and everything stops. That doesn't only apply to things like spankings either. If I'm kissing or touching you and you want it to stop, you use your safeword," he explains.

I nod in understanding. "How about 'cut'?" I suggest. "Like on a film set."

"Cut, I like that," Daddy agrees with a chuckle. "And just to be clear, I will *never* be angry if you safeword. Even if you just need a break, it's okay to use it."

"I understand," I assure him.

"Okay, then if you're ready," he says, squeezing my thigh and sitting up a little. "Stand up and strip. I want you naked so I can finally see that gorgeous body of yours." His voice drops a little lower with the command, and a shiver runs down my spine.

I scramble off his lap and do as he says, pulling my shirt off first and dropping it on the floor. I'm not sure what he'll think of my decidedly *not* twenty-year-old body, the little bit of flab around my middle, and the sprinkling of gray hairs on my chest. He rakes his eyes hungrily over me, licking his lips, making me feel like maybe there's nothing wrong with being in my forties after all.

My pants go next, leaving me standing in front of Daddy in nothing but a pair of black briefs, tented with my arousal. There's a tug in the pit of my stomach, a heat I'm not used to, but that's more than welcome.

"Come here," he says, crooking a finger at me to beckon me closer.

As soon as I'm within his reach, Daddy puts his hands on my hips, looking up at me from the couch. Even standing here, towering over him, I feel every bit of his authority, and it feels like heaven.

"You're so damn sexy," he praises, leaning forward to press a kiss to my belly, making me quiver and moan at the tenderness of the touch. My cock throbs, and the liquid heat that settles in my stomach spreads lower.

Daddy trails his mouth along my skin, over my belly, and across my chest, his hands still on my hips, his fingers teasing the waistband of my underwear but not tugging them down. When his beard tickles my peaked nipple, I gasp, my cock jerking as the sensation goes straight through me.

It's not like I'm a virgin, but damn if Daddy doesn't make me feel like no one has ever touched me before.

"Daddy," I gasp, my hips twitching of their own accord as he drags the full flat of his tongue against that same nipple. My cock leaks, soaking the fabric of my underwear, and my balls tighten.

"Daddy," I moan again, grabbing onto his broad shoulders for balance as my legs start to tremble from the feeling of his mouth on my body.

"Such a needy, responsive boy," he murmurs, grazing his teeth against my other nipple this time, causing another flood of precum. "We doing good?" he checks.

"So good," I groan. "The opposite of cut. Action, rolling, whatever the fuck will get me that spanking."

Daddy laughs, the sound vibrating against my skin. He stops playing with the waistband of my briefs, hooking his fingers in them now and yanking them down. My cock springs free, slapping my stomach and then bobbing between us.

"I've never been this hard in my life," I say breathlessly, staring down at myself in wonder. I only have a few seconds to feel self-conscious about the fact that he's likely seen dozens of perfect cocks, and I have no clue how mine measures up. The only comparisons I have are porn stars, so I'm guessing that's a fairly skewed sample.

"Your cock is gorgeous," he says before I can let any worry about it take hold. Unfortunately, that leaves me unsure what you're supposed to say when someone compliments your cock. Is thank you appropriate? I would return the compliment, but I haven't actually seen his yet, although I'm betting it probably fits right in with that skewed sample I was just thinking about.

Daddy leans back on the couch and pats his lap. "I want

you lying across my legs, ass up," he instructs firmly, stoking the flames burning me up from the inside.

I clamber somewhat awkwardly into position, folding my arms to rest my head on and then wiggling my hips around a little, first to get comfortable and then a little longer when I realize how good it feels to grind my cock against his denim-clad thigh. Damn, he has thick, strong thighs. Every inch of him is sturdy and sexy as hell.

Just like the teasing smack he gave my ass earlier, I don't see the first one coming. The slap of skin on skin resonates through the living room. I can feel the sting of the blow from my ass all the way down to my toes, and my cock jerks against his leg.

"Good boys don't squirm when they're lying over Daddy's lap."

"Sorry, Daddy," I say, even though now all I want to do is squirm.

He puts a hand on my ass cheek, and I flinch, expecting another blow, but instead he gently runs his hand along the curve until the tension eases out of my body and I start to relax again. As soon as my body is still and pliant, he draws his hand back and lands another swat. This one is much harder than the first one, reverberating through every cell in my body. My cock throbs again, and a moan falls from my lips. I arch my back, tilting my ass up to beg for more.

"My boy likes that," Daddy says, his voice dripping with warm satisfaction just before he delivers a series of rapid blows, making me gasp for breath and my balls tighten. Who knew having my bare ass spanked would get me hotter than any sex I've had in my life?

"More, Daddy," I pant.

"Shh, Daddy will take care of you," he promises, sending another bolt of arousal through me. His hand lands against my upper thigh and then right across the center of my ass, every strike making my body soar and my cock leak. "I love seeing my marks all over your skin," he murmurs.

Another jolting blow and the hot, achy feeling in the pit of my stomach starts to tighten, stealing my breath and scrambling all my thoughts. I asked Daddy before if boys ever come from being spanked, but I didn't truly believe that would happen. A few more spanks and I don't think I'll be able to *stop* it from happening. It's only the memory of Daddy's answer that keeps me holding on. He said good boys don't come unless they're told to, and Daddy didn't say I could come.

"Daddy, Daddy," I gasp, trying to find the words to ask.

He stops spanking, squeezing my cheeks again, which only intensifies the throbbing sting of my skin.

"I'm...I'm..." I groan, thrusting shamelessly against his thigh.

"Still," he commands, and I sob but obey. My body is strung tight, like a guitar string about to snap with the slightest touch. "I know you're close, baby, and you're being such a good boy. I want you to sit up and straddle me. I'm going to stroke us together. I want to feel your cock against mine when you come."

I nod, feeling almost drunk, my limbs heavy and my brain foggy as I move to do as he says. He unzips himself while I get into the position he wanted. My eyes go wide at the sight of his cock, thick and long, dark with arousal, the tip glistening with precum. There's no doubt he got as excited by the spanking as I did.

I try to imagine what it would feel like to have him inside me, stretching me open and filling me up. A moan tumbles from my lips at the mental image, his body covering mine, fully in command as he makes me feel things I've never felt before.

He works his pants down just enough to make space and then grabs my waist to tug my closer until my hard cock nudges against his. Daddy puts his hand in front of my face, offering me his palm.

"Lick for me," he says, and I obey without thinking twice about it. I run my tongue along his palm, getting it nice and wet, having fun tracing the lines with the tip of my tongue before returning to flat licks.

Once he's wet, he wraps his hand around both of our cocks, and I groan, letting my head fall against his shoulder. His cock feels so hot and hard against mine. Every quiet noise he makes courses through my body and settles in my groin. My ass is throbbing from the spanking, every blow he landed branded on my skin.

Daddy strokes us both with firm, sure strokes.

"Oh, Joey, fuck," he moans. "Kiss me, baby."

I find his lips, but the kiss is less than skillful, both of our mouths hanging open with endless sounds of pleasure. Our mouths bump against each other, sharing panting breaths as he quickens his strokes.

Daddy's free hand finds my ass again, and I gasp. My cock grows impossibly harder in his grasp, the edge of orgasm so close I can taste it.

"Can I come?" I barely manage to ask.

"You can come. Give Daddy your pleasure," he growls, and then his cock pulses against mine, coating me with hot, sticky cum. His fingers dig into the abused flesh of my ass, sending a delicious jolt of pain through me. My eyes roll back, and my balls constrict, and I'm done for. My cum joins his in covering us both, my breath comes in short bursts, and my hips twitch weakly as bliss tears through me, burning me to ash.

I collapse against Daddy, my whole body feeling like it's made of cement. He hardly even jostles me as he shuffles us into a different position, with him lying down and me contentedly blanketing him.

"What did you think?" he asks, the rise and fall of his chest soothing me as I come down from the high of my orgasm.

"I think..." I cast around for the right word to describe how incredible it felt to be with him this way. His cock is no longer hard but still absolutely huge and nudges at my thigh, and I chuckle. "I think I'm a little afraid of having you inside me but also kind of looking forward to it."

Daddy laughs, bouncing my whole body with the sound. "You know, we can always start with the other way if you don't want to dive right into the deep end."

"Seriously? You do it that way?" I ask, unable to picture it.

"Sure. Why is that so hard to believe?"

"I don't know. I can't imagine you not being in control," I admit, wrinkling my nose at the very thought.

"Oh, baby, I never said I wouldn't still be the one in charge."

I *definitely* like the sound of that.

"Come on, we're both a mess. We need a shower," he says, patting my hip with his cum-covered hand. I heave a sigh and roll off him, a smile on my lips and a happy sort of peace inside me I've never felt before.

19

DADDY

"You again?"

I don't take the greeting personally, knowing from Joey and personal experience, his dad is a bit of a curmudgeon. My boy has taken me to his dad's to officially introduce me as his boyfriend, and it's easy to see how tense he is about this. No wonder, after what he's told me about their strained relationship.

Joey's dad turns to Joey. "What is he doing here? I don't appreciate you bringing strangers to my house."

Joey sighs. "Can you let us in, Dad? I'll explain, but I would prefer to do it inside rather than standing in the doorway."

His dad shoots me another questioning glance, then steps back and opens the door wide to let us pass. We walk into the living room, and Joey points at a couch that's seen better days, where we take a seat right next to each other. His dad plops down in one of those recliner chairs, his expression sour. He doesn't offer us anything to drink, and I can feel the tension in the room. It's so sad because I don't think either of them knows how to mend the rift between them.

"Dad, this is Hunter."

"Yeah, I know. I've met him before, though why you sent him to do your job, I don't understand."

Joey looks at me, and I raise an eyebrow. I'm happy to help him in any way, but he has to take the lead here. This is one of those cases where I can't make the decisions for him.

With a quick intake of breath, Joey reaches for my hand, and we lace our fingers together. I squeeze his hand softly.

"Dad, Hunter is my boyfriend."

We both look at his father, whose mouth drops open a little before he catches himself. "Well, I guess the Christians were right, then, about the gay thing being contagious," he says. "I guess you've been hanging around gays so much you got infected."

He can't be serious, can he? I know people think shit like that, but I've never actually heard someone say it to my face.

Much to my surprise, Joey laughs, and after a few seconds, the corners of his father's mouth pull up into what looks suspiciously like a smile as well. What the hell?

Joey must've seen my puzzled expression because he turns to me and says, "It's a running joke between me and my dad that conservatives always claim kids can become queer from seeing LGBTQ characters on TV or having a transgender kid in their class or whatever."

His father shrugs. "Personally, I couldn't care less what people do in their personal lives and even less about what they do in the bedroom. It's none of my damn business, you know?"

This was not the reaction I was expecting. Then again, I never asked Joey how he thought his father would respond to him coming out, mainly because I'd gotten the impression Joey was afraid of a negative reaction. Apparently, I was wrong. Whatever caused the rift between them, it was not the *gay* part of his job.

"So," his dad says, giving me a more thorough appraisal. "His boyfriend, huh?"

"Yes, sir."

He grunts. "You can call me Herb."

I nod, though I think I'll stick with *sir* for now.

He shoots me an assessing look. "Do you have a good job, or are you planning on letting my boy pay the bills?"

I have to suppress a laugh because he couldn't be farther from the truth. "I run my own business, sir. And I can guarantee you I'm well off financially, and I have every intention of taking good care of your *boy*."

I stress the last part, and Joey squeezes my hand. That word has a completely different meaning for both of us, but obviously, that's not something he wants to share with his dad.

"He owns the studio I'm working for now," Joey says, apparently deciding to put it all out on the table. I admire it, and I'm grateful as well. I've never been a fan of hiding or keeping secrets.

Herb sighs deeply. "Of course he does. I guess your mom and I can forget about you ever doing something serious with that film degree, huh?"

Ah, there it is. That was the kind of barb I was waiting for. "I wouldn't say that, Mr. Finch. I completely understand why you've never watched any of Joey's work with the Ballsy Boys Studio, but take my word for it: it is exceptional. Did you know Ballsy Boys have won multiple awards for their cinematography? They're considered the single best gay porn studio in the country, and your son has been instrumental to their success. I'm lucky he decided to move to Vegas and come work for me."

His dad harrumphs. "Forgive me, but it's a little hard to get excited over my son doing *porn*."

I'm proud of myself for not laughing at the unintended double innuendo in that sentence. "I understand that, and twenty, thirty years ago, I'd have agreed with you. Porn used to be a seedy business that attracted a lot of less than reputable entrepreneurs. But a lot has changed, and porn right now is not only a profitable industry but also one that's become respectable. People have always watched porn, Mr. Finch, you know that. Porn is not new—hell, it's been around as long as mankind—but the Internet has made it possible to produce it much easier and distribute it much quicker and cheaper, thus giving rise to a whole new approach to porn. I'm proud of what I do, and while I understand it might not be the kind of work you thought your son would do, I hope that over time, you'll realize he's one of the best in his field."

His dad looks at me as if I'm an alien, and for a few seconds, I worry that I've gone too far with my little sermon. After all, I'm the guest here, and fueling whatever friction there is between Joey and his dad is the last thing I want to do. But then his dad's face softens, and he focuses his gaze on Joey.

"He sounds like a smart guy," he says with a jerk of his head in my direction.

"He is, Pop. He's smart and successful, and he's kind. He takes good care of me," Joey says, and that last statement warms my heart.

His dad slowly nods. "Okay," he says, and I guess that's about as positive a reaction as I could've expected. At least he didn't go off on Joey for showing up with a boyfriend rather than a girlfriend so that certainly works in his favor. And I've had worse judgments of my character than being called smart, so I'll take it.

"You gonna introduce him to your mom as well?" Herb asks, and the tension seeps back into Joey's body.

"Why would I?" Joey says, managing to sound both sad and snappy at the same time. "She doesn't even know who I am, so why would I introduce her to Hunter?"

JOEY

MY DAD'S expression goes right back to being sour. The fact that I'm dating a man was a *much* easier topic for us to discuss than my mother is.

"That's your mother. You'd better show her some respect," my dad growls.

I dip my head, feeling ashamed and angry all at once. *I* need to show her respect? He hasn't even gone to visit her. I moved back here to make sure they were both taken care of, and he can't be bothered to spend ten minutes in the car with me to see his wife. I rearranged my life and have stressed myself to the max, bending over backward for both of them. Does he think I *like* going to visit her and never having her even know who I am? Is all this supposed to be fun for me?

I open my mouth to tell him just that, but Daddy puts his hand on the back of my neck, giving it a small squeeze, which draws me up short. Those few extra seconds are all I need to realize that saying something so hurtful isn't going to do anything to help either of us.

"You're right. I shouldn't have said that," I concede, and

my dad looks surprised. "It would be nice to introduce Hunter to mom. Would you like to come with us?"

He shifts in his seat, appearing uncomfortable. "I don't think I want to see her like that," he confesses.

"I understand. But think about it, okay? Because even if she can't remember much, I think it still makes her happy to have visitors. She's still Mom."

He grunts in acknowledgment but doesn't say anything else. I guess that's better than nothing, and I didn't even get anything thrown at me, so I'd call this visit a win.

"It was nice to see you again, Mr. Finch," Hunter says, standing up and offering my dad his hand. "You've still got my number in case you need anything, right?"

My dad nods but remains silent. Again, better than being outright shitty, so I'll take it.

"I'll see you again in a few days, Dad. If you need anything in the meantime, just call," I say.

"Thanks, son." I smile, leaning against Daddy and doing a little happy dance inside. We still have a hell of a long way to go, but this felt like a step in the right direction.

"That went well," Daddy says after we step outside.

"It did," I agree. "That's the longest conversation my dad and I have had since my mom got sick."

"I'm glad. And I really would like to meet your mom. I know she won't remember, but I'd still like it."

"I know," I say. "Let's go. There are still a few hours left for visiting."

He helps me into the car as always, and then I direct him to the memory care facility.

Julie is behind the desk again, and she greets me happily. Over the past couple of months, I've gotten to know most of the staff, and it's only made me more frustrated that my dad won't come visit. I know he's imagining that she's locked away somewhere horrible, but this is the nicest place I could afford, probably one of the best facilities in Vegas.

"Hi, Joey. How are you doing today?"

"I'm good. How are you?" I ask as I quickly fill out the visitor log.

"Can't complain," she responds with a giggle.

"I brought my boyfriend to meet my mom today. Wish me luck."

"Oh, that's so sweet. Good luck."

I take Daddy's hand and lead him back toward the main room, where my mom spends most of the day, part of me hoping she's having one of her rare good days where she'll recognize me, the other part refusing to hope for anything so I can't be disappointed.

I find her sitting at a round table, working on what looks like a simple puzzle. Her eyes light up when she sees me, which is a good sign.

"Joey," she says my name with so much happiness my heart nearly bursts. "How was school today?" My shoulders sag. Knowing who I am is still a good day, right?

"It was good, Mom," I say, leaning over to kiss her on the cheek. "Looks like you're working on something fun."

She looks down at the puzzle with confusion like she's never seen it before.

"Mom, there's someone I want you to meet," I say. She looks back up at me and then over at Daddy. "This is Hunter. He's my boyfriend."

"Of course, I know Hunter," she says, waving me away like I'm talking nonsense. I look over at Daddy and give him a weak shrug, hoping he understands that she's obviously not herself anymore.

"That's right. We go way back," Hunter plays along,

sliding onto the seat beside her, facing the table. "You want to help me with this puzzle? It looks like a doozy."

She smiles and reaches for one of the puzzle pieces. I grab one of the other seats, and the three of us spend the afternoon working on the puzzle and listening to my mom tell stories from her childhood. Although I think some of them were actually episodes of *Little House on the Prairie*, but close enough, I guess.

When visiting hours end, we both give my mom a hug, and Hunter promises her we'll visit again soon.

"You were so good with her, thank you." I lean against him as we walk out to the car.

"She's sweet, but am I imagining things, or were some of her stories actually from TV shows?"

"They definitely were." I let out a small laugh. Even if she likely won't remember him tomorrow, I'm glad I brought him to meet her. She might not know it, but she was happy today, we had fun, and that's what's important.

My stomach growls, and Daddy kisses the top of my head. "Let's go get some dinner, and then I say we spend the rest of the night cuddling in front of the TV."

"That sounds perfect, Daddy," I agree with a happy sigh.

20

DADDY

When Joey opens the door, he's dressed exactly like I told him to. As much as I love the way he fills a pair of jeans, sweatpants are easier for what I have in mind for us.

"Hi, Daddy," Joey says with a happy undertone.

I step inside and close the door behind me. Even though we'll leave in a few minutes, I want to take my time greeting my boy, and I need no spectators for that. Besides, I'm hoping to do a little more than kissing so he won't accidentally *embarrass* himself later.

Instead of saying words, I simply wrap my arms around him and pull him against me. We'll start with a hug because I know how much those mean to my boy. Joey crawls against me, immediately surrendering to his need for touch. It never ceases to amaze me how natural he feels in my arms, even though he's so different from any other boy I've ever had. I let my cheek rest on the top of his head, murmuring sweet words while my hands slip under his T-shirt and rub his back.

We stand for at least two minutes like this, Joey

completely calm, just standing there and enjoying being held. I lift my hands and gently tilt his head back so I can kiss him. As always, I set a slow pace, not wanting to miss any kind of signal he's not ready or that he doesn't want it, but he opens up for me instantly.

He tastes sweet, with a hint of chocolate, so he must have been snacking again. I make a mental note to check his refrigerator and make sure he has some healthy snacks as well as a few ready-to-eat meals that aren't pure sugar and carbs. Of course, this would all be far easier if he moved in with me, but that's not a thought I'll speak out loud anytime soon. I'd love having him in my bed, but slow is the mantra here. I can't rush this.

He's eager to kiss me back, making soft noises when I lick into his mouth, then gently nibble on his bottom lip. I love the way he sighs, an almost innocent expression of how much he is into this. As professional as he is on the job, his reactions in private are far more unguarded. Pure. It's like he's showing me a part that nobody else gets to see, and I can't help but like that with a possessiveness that's a little frightening.

I angle my head to get my tongue deeper into his mouth, since Joey is giving all signals he's more than on board with this. All it takes is a few steps forward for me, and Joey is with his back against the wall with me boxing him in, slowly pressing our groins together. He's hard, which makes me both happy and relieved because it tells me he's truly enjoying this and not merely doing it to please me.

Our difference in height is minimal, which allows me to rub our dicks together, even with a few layers of clothing in between. Joey makes a beautiful sound, something like a grunt mixed in with a sigh and a keening noise I've never heard him make before.

And so I keep kissing him, seeking friction against him until my cock is leaking like crazy. I'd hoped we'd get to do this before we left, and I arrived earlier on purpose just in case, which means I can take my time with him. I break off the kiss long enough to make eye contact with him as I slip my hand behind the waistband of his boxers, waiting a beat or two to give him time to say no.

"Please, Daddy," he whispers instead, his voice filled with need.

"What do you want Daddy to do, boy? Do you want me to jerk us off together again?"

I take my cock out as well and spread both of our precum around to make it slick enough to grab us together in my hand. Joey lets his head fall back against the wall, his eyes closed and his mouth slightly open. His moan increases when I fist us slowly, and I love the expression of pleasure on his face.

"Or would you like to feel Daddy's mouth on you?"

Joey's eyes fly open, and he rights his head to meet my eyes. I see him swallow before he says, "Yes?"

It sounds like a question, not a statement of consent, and that will not do. "Was that a yes, boy? Or do we need to slow down?"

"No! No slowing down, I mean," Joey says. "Daddy." He then adds quickly, "It was a yes. To the..."

He stumbles over the word, and I grin. "You must have filmed thousands of these, boy. Yet when it's you, you can't bring yourself to say the word blow job?"

Joey's cheeks get that lovely red hue. "You didn't use that word either, Daddy," he fires back, and I have to give him props for his quick repartee under these circumstances.

"Fair enough. But if you want Daddy to suck your dick, you're gonna have to ask me. Nicely."

How is it possible that someone who has worked in the porn industry for so long can still be so innocent? I can't explain it, but I love it. He has no trouble filming whatever debauched scene plays in front of him, but when it's him, he gets all flustered and awkward.

He swallows again, but his jaw sets in determination, so I know he won't back down from this challenge. "Daddy," he says, and his voice is soft but steady. "Would you please put your mouth on my cock?"

I claim his mouth in another kiss, needing to taste him again, but then I let go of him and slowly lower myself to my knees. There was a time when I could do this without a second thought, but I've reached the age where dropping my full weight on my knees like that is not a good idea. Instead, I use my arms to spread my weight. It makes my descent a little less elegant but a hell of a lot easier on my body, and at the end of the day, I'll take comfort over gracefulness, thank you very much.

Joey doesn't seem to care either, since he looks down on me with a gaze that makes my heart flutter in my chest. I smile at him, then take his cock in my right hand and give the tip a quick lick to catch the fat drop of precum. I've seen his dick the first time I jerked us off together, right after he'd taken his first spanking so beautifully, but it's my first taste of him, and I let it roll around my tongue before I swallow.

I look up at him. "Tell me your safeword, boy."

His response is immediate, which reassures me that he'll use it when he has to. "Cut."

I nod in response, then keep eye contact with him as I take the head of his cock into my mouth. I trace it with my tongue, wanting to get to know him, and Joey lets out a low moan. I take my time exploring his shape, the soft ridges, testing how sensitive he is. When I suck the head into my mouth and put a little suction on it, Joey makes another beautiful sound.

He also instinctively bucks into my mouth, so I bring up my left hand to hold his base. Despite trying hard over the years, I've never been able to completely eliminate my gag reflex, and I want to prevent him from triggering it on the first time I'm blowing him.

"Sorry, Daddy," he says, his voice filled with remorse.

I let his cock slip out of my mouth with a wet plop. "No need to apologize. You did nothing wrong, boy. I'll set the limits, remember? If you do something wrong, I will tell you, and until I do, you don't need to worry. That's my job."

He nods, and once I've assured myself that he really understands, I go back to what I was doing, sucking in his cock a little deeper. He's not long, but he's got girth, which actually works out fine for me, since he's not as likely to hit the back of my throat. And man, I do love the sensation of having my mouth stuffed full of cock. I've always been a fan of a little breath play during blow jobs, both on the giving as on the receiving end.

Joey fills my mouth for sure, and once I've explored the rest of him with my tongue, it's time to get to work. I take him in as far as I can, resulting in him trying to push into my mouth again, but my left hand prevents it. Once I know he'll hold steady, I make slow moves with my left hand while sucking him. My right hand wraps around my cock, which I start working in the same rhythm.

I hum with pleasure, my mouth full of him and his taste, and my arousal is building up fast. So is his, from the sounds of it, as he's switched from the occasional grunt and moan to a litany of gorgeous sounds, all these words and noises that encourage me to keep going. His hands weave into my hair, and he pulls tightly, with just the right amount of pressure.

"I'm close," he warns me, but I have no intention of letting go. I do pull back a little. I always think it's a waste to let someone come straight down your throat because that way, you can barely taste them. Call me weird, but I actually love the taste of cum.

My right hand moves faster as I start to chase my orgasm, and my balls are tight and heavy, my spine tingling as my muscles start to tense up.

"Daddy," Joey moans, and then louder, "Daddy!"

I stop jerking myself off, not wanting to distract myself so I can focus completely on him. He floods my mouth as he comes with a loud grunt, spurting out so much cum at once that I can barely keep up. I swallow quickly, then let the second mouthful linger on my tongue a little longer. Some of it trickles down my chin, but I couldn't care less.

Joey's body relaxed, I resume jacking myself off, and with three hard squeezes, I fill my hand with my release. God, that was good. I've always loved the overload of sensations when you make someone else come while you orgasm at the same time. It's this explosion of nerves in your body, and there's nothing like it.

As soon as I let go of Joey, he sinks to the floor on his bare ass, his pants still halfway down his legs. He looks at me with heavy eyes, his lips still swollen from our kissing and his cheeks all rosy. He smiles at me, then reaches for my face and swipes something off my chin. Without thinking, I open my mouth, and he lets out a little gasp as he pushes his thumb between my lips. I can taste the last traces of him on his thumb, and I circle it thoroughly with my tongue to get every last drop off.

"That was...perfect," Joey says, and I reposition myself on

my butt as well—though I do pull up my pants because that floor is way too cold on my ass—so I can draw him to my side and make him lean against me.

"Yeah? Was that what you had imagined it would be?"

He nods. "All actually, it surpassed my expectations. Don't forget that the bar was pretty low, considering how unenthusiastic I've been about my previous experiences with sex. I mean, it was okay-ish, but nothing like this."

That honest review makes me laugh. "So what you're saying that even if this was a relatively bad blow job, you wouldn't know anyway, since you had little to compare it to?"

Joey chuckles as well. "Well, I wouldn't have put it quite like that, but I guess you're right."

"I'll have to do this far more often, then, so you actually can compare."

"I fully support that proposal," Joey says, and then we both laugh again.

A few minutes later, I've cleaned both of us up, and we're ready to leave. "Where are you taking me today that I have to dress like this?" Joey asks. "And not only me, but you're dressed pretty casually as well."

I do a check to make sure there's nothing visible of our *previous activities*, and then give him a last kiss on his mouth. "We are going to get a massage."

21

JOEY

By the time we pull up in front of the spa, I'm still all loose and relaxed from the blow job. I wasn't lying when I said all the blow jobs I've had before have been pretty unexciting. Don't get me wrong. They weren't *bad* per se, but I often found myself thinking about other things or, more often, feeling bad and worrying I was taking too long to finish. With Daddy, I don't think about *anything* else when he's touching me. He commands all my attention and takes away all my worries. If he wanted me to finish faster, then I have no doubt he could have made that happen. It's a liberating feeling, knowing all I have to do is enjoy whatever he's giving me.

"I've never had a massage before," I admit, taking Daddy's hand when he holds it out to help me out of the car.

"Never?" he asks with surprise. "But you lug around heavy equipment all day."

I shrug. "I guess I never thought about it."

"This is going to be life changing, then," he declares with a grin. I'm pretty sure every moment with Daddy so far has been life changing, but that's *way* too cheesy to say out loud, so instead I just smile and let him lead me inside.

We check in, and the perky red-haired receptionist behind the desk offers us cucumber water, which is something I'm proud to say I've never heard of before. Then she shows us back to a room set up for a couples massage with two massage tables and leaves us to get undressed, telling us our massage therapists will be in shortly.

"If you've never had a massage before, I suppose I should've asked you if you're comfortable with touch."

Warm affection floods through me as I take my shirt off and fold it neatly. "I love how much you're always worrying about me."

"I'm your Daddy. It's my job," he says simply.

"I appreciate it. I'm good with touch," I assure him. "I love it, in fact. This is probably going to sound exceedingly strange, but have you ever heard of cuddle clubs?"

"*Cuddle* clubs?" he repeats, raising his eyebrows at me as he undresses as well.

"Yeah, it's where a group of people get together and just cuddle," I explain.

"I can't say I've ever heard of that, but it sounds nice. Have you gone to one?"

"No." I shake my head, blushing a little. "I was part of this Facebook group for a while, though, back in LA, and I always thought about going. I always found an excuse or told myself I was too busy when the monthly meetup would get scheduled, but I thought about it a lot. I've been single for a long time now, and cuddling is the thing I miss the most."

Daddy wraps his arms around me. We're both down to only our boxers now, and his body feels nice against mine, comforting without any hint of demanding. I press my cheek against his warm skin and take a deep, relaxing breath. I think I'm falling in love with him, but it has to be way too soon for that, right?

There's a light knock on the door, and Daddy gives me a quick kiss on the forehead before releasing me.

"One second," he calls out, and we both get comfortable on our tables.

The massage itself is unbelievable—soothing music, lavender-scented oil, and a pair of strong hands expertly working out knots in my shoulders I didn't even know were there. The best part, though, by far is the occasional sound of Daddy's quiet moans.

When his masseur hits just the right spot, there's a gasp and then a muffled sound of pleasure, and every time it happens my cock gets harder. The longer it goes on, the surer I am of one thing. *I* want to be the one to draw those sounds from him. Good boys suck cock, right? If not, then maybe I want to be a naughty boy just this once...well, probably more than once, but we'll see how the first time goes.

I roll my shoulders and groan after the massage therapists leave us to get dressed.

"Oh my god, I feel like a new man." I sigh happily.

"Glad to hear it." Daddy grins. "You're going to feel like you got hit by a bus tomorrow, though, before it feels good again, so be sure to drink plenty of water today."

"Yes, Daddy," I agree. "Hey, could we swing by the studio real quick?" I ask, keeping my face neutral so he doesn't catch on to my dirty plan.

"Sure. Do you need to pick something up?"

"Mmhmm," I mumble. It's not a real lie if I don't actually say words, right? Besides, this is the fun kind of lie that I'm sure Daddy won't mind.

"If you tell me what you need, I could run in and grab it

for you," he offers when we pull up into the empty parking lot of Kinky Boys Studios.

"I'll go in. You can come with me, though," I say, already knowing he'll want to come with me.

Once we get inside, I head over to the nearest soundstage—the bedroom set—and turn on the main light for the set.

"What are you doing?" Daddy asks.

"Nothing, Daddy," I say innocently. "Will you sit on the bed for me for a second?"

I get a quirked eyebrow from him, but he walks over to the bed and sits down. I left my camera set up last night after we filmed an introduction video for Glam, so all I have to do is turn it on.

"Is it okay if I film you, Daddy?" I ask sweetly. Maybe this boy thing is easier to get the hang of than I thought it would be.

"Film me doing what?" he asks, his voice a deep purr. He's onto me, and he seems on board to play along.

"Getting a return on the favor you gave me at my apartment earlier," I confess with a grin, still feeling a little awkward to say the word blow job out loud. "Since it's my first time and all, I thought it might be good to have it on film so I can study it later and improve on my technique."

He seems to take a few seconds to think it over before a dirty smile stretches over his lips, and he nods. "Turn it on."

I do as he says, checking the framing and then making my way over to him. I wish I could film the whole thing myself and really capture the moment properly, but a stationary shot will have to do. Either way, I have a feeling this will be something Daddy will want to watch over and over.

When I reach the bed, I drop to my knees—padded

flooring for the win. That was a genius move on Daddy's part when he had the sets built up together—and gaze up at Daddy, unleashing the full force of my feelings in my eyes. He's given me so much in such a short time. I can't believe how lucky I am. He's shown me a part of myself I never knew existed, and taken such good care of me. Even before he became my Daddy, he was taking care of me. My heart feels so full that I don't know how my chest contains it.

Everything makes so much sense now in a way it never has before. Yes, taking Daddy's cock into my mouth and sucking him until he comes *is* as mechanical and frankly strange as I always thought sex was. But using this act to show Daddy how I feel about him, using it to give him pleasure the way he's given it to me...there's nothing mechanical or strange about that. It's beautiful.

"Oh, my sweet boy," Daddy says, looking down at me with as much adoration as I feel. He cups the side of my jaw and strokes his thumb along the curve of my cheek. "You want Daddy's cock?" he asks, and an excited shiver runs down my spine.

"Yes, Daddy," I answer without hesitation, reaching for the zipper of his jeans and tugging them open. He lifts his hips to shove his jeans and boxers down. He looks even bigger from this vantage point than he did when he jerked us both off, but I'm not as intimidated as I expected to be. Daddy won't let me do this wrong. He'll help me and tell me how to make him feel good.

He wraps a hand around the base of his cock and strokes himself slowly, making the veins stand out more prominently and a clear bead of precum form on his slit. I lick my lips, watching with wonder as he touches himself. I tremble in my spot, waiting impatiently for his instructions.

"You won't be able to safeword, so if you need me to stop, tap my thigh."

"Yes, Daddy."

"Good boy. Now open your mouth," he says gruffly, and I obey instantly, parting my lips but staying in place. "Such a good boy," Daddy groans, running the fingers of his free hand through my hair and pulling me closer. He keeps jacking himself, dragging the head of his cock along my bottom lip. It feels hot and smooth, the salty taste of his precum hitting my tongue. "You like Daddy's cock?"

"Mmhmm," I murmur, trying to nod, but his grasp on my hair tightens, reminding me he's holding me in place. A jolt of lust sparks in my gut, and I moan against the tip of his cock.

"Give it a kiss."

I moan again, letting my eyes fall closed for just a second as I kiss the head of his cock with a filthy, open-mouthed, tongue-heavy kiss. He groans, and when I open my eyes again, his head is tilted back, and his chest rises and falls with rapid breaths.

"Open a little wider," he instructs once he catches his breath, returning his heated gaze to my face with a hungry expression. I open my mouth as wide as I can, and he pushes the first few inches inside.

I stroke my tongue along the underside of his erection, feeling every throbbing vein. My lips are stretched wide around his hefty girth, and I can't believe how incredibly *hard* he feels. For the second time, I imagine what it would feel like for him to stretch and fill my ass. I whimper around him, and his hips twitch, and another moan rumbles through him.

I've never given any thought to what it would be like to have a man's cock in my mouth like this, but for the look on

Daddy's face alone, I'd be happy to do this every day for the rest of our lives.

He rocks his hips gently, pushing only a few inches in before drawing back. He's being careful with me, and as much as I appreciate that he's always taking care of me, right now, I want him to let go a little and use me for his pleasure.

On his next thrust, I push my head forward, ignoring the sting of my scalp as he tries to hold me in place. I hum happily at the fullness, the slight ache in my jaw, the taste of him on my tongue.

"So greedy," he groans, and it doesn't sound the least bit like a complaint. "You want more? You want it rougher?" The question seems to be rhetorical because he starts thrusting deeper immediately. My eyelids flutter closed, and I suck eagerly. The thick head of his cock hits the back of my throat, and I gag, but he doesn't let up. I swallow around his cock, which isn't an easy feat, and try to relax. I gag the second time as well, but the third time he presses against the back of my throat, I manage to take him deeper.

Daddy lets out a deep, gasping growl and holds his cock there, cutting me off from breathing. Even with him completely in control of my oxygen intake, I can't find a shred of panic inside myself. I could tap him if I really needed to, but I trust him to know when I'll need to breathe again.

When he pulls out again, I drag in a ragged breath through my nose, my throat burning from the stretch, drool coating my chin. Tears roll down my cheeks too, and I'm sure I look like a mess. But the expression of hungry awe on Daddy's face before he thrusts in again is all I need.

The bed squeaks and groans under his thrusts, and something about the sound is erotic as hell. Daddy fucks my throat with abandon, praise and moans falling from his lips as his thrusts grow faster, more desperate. The only warning I get before his cum floods my mouth is the thickening of his cock and a shout of pleasure.

I swallow as fast as I can, not wanting to waste a drop of what he's giving me. Pulse after pulse of hot, salty cum lands on my tongue, and I moan with each one. Even when they stop coming, I keep sucking and licking, wanting every last drop of what Daddy has to give me. I only stop once he pulls me off his cock.

I gasp for breath, licking my damp lips and still gazing up at Daddy, who looks satisfyingly wrecked and happy all at once.

"Did I do good, Daddy?" I ask, my voice coming out raspy from the rough treatment.

"You did *very* good. Come here and lie with Daddy for a minute." He pats the bed, and I crawl up to lie down beside him, resting my head on his chest. I forgot about the camera rolling for a second, but when I remember it, I feel even happier, knowing I'll have our post-blow job cuddle on film as well.

I snuggle close to him and close my eyes, trying and failing to think of a single moment in my life when I've been happier.

22
DADDY

My parents were always big on Christmas when I was growing up. Decorating the tree and hanging up all the Christmas lights outside was a family tradition the weekend after Thanksgiving. It was my favorite time of the year, though of course, getting presents played a massive role in that.

My parents took those seriously as well. I remember being amazed at how accurately Santa had guessed what we would like to get, until I discovered the truth. Funny enough, it didn't make it less of a miracle for me. My parents are far from perfect, but they sure gave us kids everything they could.

It made Christmas morning the best morning of the year. We would get up, way too early, only to be sent back to bed by my exasperated parents at least twice before we were finally allowed downstairs. And then when we were, we'd all gasp at the stacks of colorful presents under the tree. My mom would make us all hot chocolate with whipped cream, and then we'd unwrap the presents, each waiting our turn so we could cheer with each other for whatever someone else got.

That excitement, that happy, bubbly feeling in your stomach when you know something amazing is about to happen, that's exactly how I feel right now. Today is the launch party for Kinky Boys, and I am equal parts excited and terrified. It's been one hell of a ride the last few months, and there have been times when I doubted if everything would ever come together. Now that it finally has, it's hard to believe that it's about to become real.

I considered holding it at an outside accommodation, like a hotel ballroom or some party center, but then decided against it. One of the things Bear impressed upon me was the importance of facilitating close relationships between the boys, and I don't see that happening if we have our events in public. Bear said he'd always try to do as much as possible at the studio, so that's what I ended up doing as well.

I do a last check, slowly walking around the main floor, which has been transformed into something resembling a party room. I rented tables and chairs, Joey helped me pick out some decorations—though we agreed they're fairly cheesy—and I've arranged for a catering company to take care of food and drinks.

"Daddy, I'm here!" Joey calls out, and I rush toward the sound of his voice, as always excited to see him, even though it's only been an hour since he left the studio to grab some extra snacks to put on the tables. I told him the catering company would provide all the food, but he wasn't happy with the snacks they'd listed on their quote. Something about them being too healthy. I don't know. It sounds like him, that's for sure. Joey and healthy are not exactly synonymous.

"Hey, baby," I say, then kiss him soundly. "Did you get everything you wanted?"

Joey nods, holding up two grocery bags. "A couple of different kinds of chips, pretzel sticks, and M&Ms. I got us covered."

I open my mouth to comment on the choice of M&Ms, then decide I really don't care enough, and close it again. He pops open some of the bags he brought and puts a little bit of everything on every table. The guy from the catering company sends me a look with a raised eyebrow, and I shrug. The contract didn't state we couldn't bring our own food as well, so whatever.

When Joey's finished dividing the snacks, he steps up to me, and I pull him close to my side.

"Are you excited, Daddy?" he asks.

"If you want to label this churning in my stomach, my clammy hands, and my racing heart excitement, then let's go with that. Personally, I'd call it being terrified, but what do I know?"

Joey grins. "At least you haven't lost your sense of humor. I told you it will be awesome. You've assembled a great team."

My heart warms at that praise. "We have assembled a great team," I gently correct him. "This is as much your doing as it is mine, baby."

He looks up at me with a mix of happiness and surprise. "Thank you. I'm proud to be a part of this."

Whatever I want to say is interrupted when the front door opens, and a familiar voice calls out, "Hello! Anyone home?"

My eyes widen in surprise as I look at Joey. "Did you know about this?"

Joey merely laughs, which gives him away. "You and I

will have a discussion later about keeping things from your Daddy, boy," I fake-admonish him, and he laughs even more.

"We're here!" I shout, and seconds later, Bear steps into the room, Pixie by his side. I let go of Joey and hurry over toward them. Bear pulls me into a tight hug.

"Thank you for coming," I say. "It's a big surprise, but a very welcome one. I had no idea you'd be here."

Bear chuckles, then releases me. "Joey here is good at keeping secrets." He winks at Joey, who manages to look deceivingly innocent.

"Hi, Daddy," Pixie singsongs to me, then giggles. "This is going to be confusing to call both of you Daddy."

Bear grabs him by the neck. "It won't be, baby boy, because the only man you'll be calling Daddy is me. You can call him Hunter, like everyone else."

"*I* call him Daddy," Joey quips, and the easy, casual way he affirms our relationship in front of his former boss makes my heart sing.

"You and I need to have a talk," Pixie tells him, his eyes sparkling as he stabs Joey on his chest with a finger. "Because you've been holding out on us about wanting a Daddy, and I asked Daddy for details, and he wouldn't say anything. Something about you having a right to privacy, which we both know is total bullshit."

God, I love that kid. Bear has his hands full with him, but it's clear he doesn't mind. It's funny because once upon a time, I might've been slightly jealous. Hell, once upon a time, I entertained the thought of pursuing Pixie for myself. Granted, that was before I knew how Bear felt about him, but the attraction was there. And yet as I look at him now, all I feel is a warm, protective kind of love, like an older brother or a dad. It's nothing compared to this intense feeling I have whenever I look at Joey.

I hug Pixie, kissing the top of his head. "Don't ever change, little imp. You are good for this grumpy old bastard."

I let go of him, and he gives me a thorough once-over. "You look different than you did before," he says. "Happier. More relaxed."

Cheesy as it is, I point at Joey. "That's all him. He makes me happy."

"Aw..." Pixie says, getting those starry eyes, and Joey moans with embarrassment.

The front door opens again, and I hear more voices and footsteps coming in. I check my watch. They're right on time.

"Come, let me introduce you to my team," I tell Bear, my voice ringing with pride.

JOEY

HAVING ALL the cast in the same room for the first time makes it feel truly real. All the guys seem a little starstruck by Bear and Pixie at first, but that wears off by the time the food is served.

A sense of pride fills me, watching all the guys interact. The fast and easy camaraderie reminds me a lot of the Ballsy Boys, and I couldn't be happier about that. I know this is Daddy's studio, but I feel like it's a little bit mine too.

Glam and Ian seem to click immediately, both swooping in on Byron, who was looking a little awkward, standing off to one side by himself, and making him feel welcome. I never realized how simple it would be to pick out the Doms from the subs in the room. Harley is a lot like Bear and Daddy, standing with his shoulders squared, radiating an air of confident authority. I notice Max is giving off a similar vibe, but he seems a lot less sure of himself.

Since the game of *Spot the Dom* is such fun, I let my eyes roam over the film and backstage crew as well, seeing if I can guess what they are, if they're even in the lifestyle at all, that is.

I notice Silas with a drink in his hand, his eyes trained on Ian with a spark of interest. If I were behind my camera, I would zoom in on the intense expression that flashes across his face for a second before he covers it with a look of indifference. *Interesting.* He *definitely* has a Dom vibe going.

I look back over at Ian to see if he notices Silas's attention at all, and I find Harley throwing his arm around the sub's shoulders. He says something that makes Ian throw his head back and laugh. Silas's face turns stormy, and he takes another sip of his drink before turning away from watching the group and pretends to be busy with something. *Interesting.*

The party is in full swing when another man I've never met before shows up. He looks like he's about Daddy's age, and I would bet my whole paycheck on him being a Dom too. He swaggers in with a grin on his face, heading straight for Daddy. They greet each other with a back-slapping hug.

"Joey, come here for a second," Daddy calls me over. "This is Marshall. He's a friend from New York. I've hired him as a scene consultant. Marshall, this is our head cameraman and my boy, Joey." There's so much pride in Daddy's voice when he calls me his boy I nearly turn into a pile of goo on the spot.

"It's nice to meet you," I say, offering my hand to Marshall.

"Come on, I'll introduce you to the talent, and then you can grab something to eat and mingle."

Each of the subs eye Marshall with interest as he's introduced, except Byron, who seems to shrink a little, blushing and then spilling his drink when he fumbles to shake Marshall's hand.

"Hey." Pixie sidles up to me with a mischievous grin, which is pretty much Pixie's default expression. "Come sneak away with me for a few minutes. I *need* all the juicy details."

I chuckle. "Why do we have to sneak?"

"Because my Daddy told me not to pry so we can't let him catch us before we get away," he explains in a conspiratorial whisper.

"What'll he do if he catches you?" I ask with amusement.

"Probably spank me." He doesn't seem all that concerned by the prospect. "So I guess it's mostly a win-win, but I'd rather get the dirty details before I get my spanking if I can help it."

"Okay, come on. I know where we can go." I tilt my head to show him which direction to follow me, and we quietly slip out of the party area. I lead him through the dark part of the studio over to the locker room set, which should be far enough away from the party to sit and talk for a little while without being discovered.

Pixie straddles one of the benches and sits down. It's no wonder the boy was such a hit for Ballsy Boys. Even sitting here fully clothed, he looks like he's waiting for someone to come through the door and fuck him.

"These sets are fantastic. I can't wait to watch the videos," he says, looking around at the lockers with interest. I plop down onto the bench next to him, but I skip the porn star theatrics and simply sit down like any normal person would. "So, was Hunter just so hot he woke up your latent bisexuality or what?"

I snort a laugh. "As gorgeous as he is, it didn't have anything to do with that. I mean, I've watched attractive men fuck each other's brains out for years and never had so much as a twitch of interest down south."

"That's fair. I mean, if Tank and Brewer's first scene together didn't give you a raging boner, I imagine it would take someone pretty special to do it."

"Yeah," I agree, clearing my throat. I know I don't *have* to come out to Pixie. He's not even being particularly pushy. I'm sure if I segue into more spanking talk, he won't complain, but I want to see how it feels to say it out loud to someone aside from Daddy, and this is as safe a space as I'm going to get. "I'm pretty sure I'm demisexual and probably panromantic."

"Cool," he says simply. "It was totally the Daddy stuff that got you, then, right?" he goes on, hardly even blinking at my admission.

"It was absolutely the Daddy stuff," I say with a grin. "It's difficult not to like someone who's always being so caring and sweet to you. And the liking led to a connection, and the connection led to...well, you know." My cheeks warm. I've filmed this man getting DP'd, and somehow I *still* feel weird talking about my own sex life in front of him.

"Epic sex?" he guesses.

"Pretty epic, yeah," I say with a laugh.

"You love him?" he asks.

"Yeah, I really do," I answer, my stomach fluttering because I still haven't told Daddy himself yet.

Pixie sighs happily, putting a hand over his heart with a dreamy look in his eyes. "Isn't love the best?"

"It absolutely is."

"Oh my god, you know what we should do?" he asks, sitting up straighter, his face full of excitement and impishness.

"I'm a little afraid to ask."

"We should try to pair up the new cast, be little matchmakers so they all fall in love too."

I throw my head back and laugh. "I think I saw a few sparks flying already. It's probably best to let them all work that out among themselves."

"Oh, tell me who."

We're still gossiping and laughing when Daddy and Bear find us a little while later. Bear throws Pixie over his shoulder, admonishing him for being bad and sneaking off, but the grin on Pixie's face tells me it's all going as he hoped. He waves at me as Bear carries him away.

"Pretty good party," I tell Daddy, standing up and wrapping my arms around him.

"It's a great party," he agrees. "It feels like the cast is clicking well. I think we're going to do something special here."

"I know we will."

"Come on, I've got a little speech planned, and then I want to hit the button to set the first video to be live while everyone is here watching," he says, taking my hand and leading me back out to the party.

"Can I have everyone's attention, please," he calls out in a booming voice, the din of the party quieting in an instant. *God, it's so hot when he's in charge.*

"Speech," Ian says teasingly, and Daddy chuckles.

"Yes, you all have to sit through a short speech, and my guess is it will be the first of many because I can't deny I enjoy the sound of my own voice from time to time," he jokes, and a titter of laughter goes through the room. "I just want to say that I feel lucky that so many of you are willing to take a chance on an unknown studio. Most of you are here because of the Ballsy Boys name or my amazing cameraman and boyfriend, Joey, but it means a lot to me. I know I've talked your ears off already about what this studio means to me and why it's so important to me to have a place where viewers can learn about safe, consensual kink and have a good time doing it, and I couldn't do any of this without all of you. I'm really looking forward to what the future has to hold for the Kinky Boys."

"Here, here," Marshall says, raising his plastic cup. Everyone else follows suit, toasting to the Kinky Boys.

"And now it's time to officially press the button on our first video," Daddy says. "Sheldon, where are you?" He squints through the small crowd in search of our tech guy, who raises his hand and shuffles to the front with his tablet in hand. When I was playing my *Dom vs sub* game earlier, I totally pegged Sheldon as a sub. A cute one too, but that's neither here nor there.

Sheldon's fingers fly over his screen for a few seconds, pausing for a moment to push his glasses higher on his nose, and then he grins and holds the tablet out for Daddy. "All you have to do is press that button, and Bear and Pixie's scene will go live."

Daddy hits the button.

"The Kinky Boys are officially live," Daddy declares, and everyone cheers.

23

DADDY

I've always loved sex. In fact, ever since my first experience with sex at the tender age of fourteen—yes, I was an early bloomer—I've always been sexually active. And in certain periods of my life *active* was an understatement because I fucked someone every day, if not more often. I guess that kind of comes with the territory when you own a club, but I loved it.

Sex has also always been a crucial part of being a Daddy. Of course it's not all about the sex. At the very core, being a Daddy is about taking care of my boy and providing him with whatever he needs. It just so happens that most boys I've had so far—come to think of it, all of them—were equally interested in sex as I was.

And there's the crucial word. *Was.*

I've thought about it, and this is the longest in my life I've ever gone without sex. We could argue about the definition of sex, so let's use the infamous definition of President Clinton and consider oral sex and hand jobs not sex.

They are, obviously, but I've never liked the term anal sex. The word *anal* has such a negative connotation, one that couldn't be further from the truth when it comes to sex. There's nothing anal about anal sex, and if that statement sounds confusing, my apologies because it made a whole of a lot more sense in my head.

The point is that Joey and I have grown very close, and I've loved every moment I got to spend with him. And it wasn't until today that I realized that I don't miss it. The sex. Or pertaining to my previous statement, anal sex. We haven't done *it*, and I can't believe I'm saying this, but I don't miss it.

Now, would I love to go *all the way*, to use an old-fashioned expression, with Joey? Hell, yes. Am I impatient for it? No. When we started seeing each other and he told me he was demisexual, I had counted on this being a challenge for me. Not a problem, mind you, but a challenge for sure. After all, at the risk of repeating myself, sex has always been such an integral part of my life, of my relationships, that I figured that to not have that would be difficult. Turns out, it's been surprisingly easy.

Joey has been giving signals that he's ready for more, but I want him to take his time. I don't ever want him to look back and feel like he rushed things, that I put pressure on him, that he felt obligated to take a step he wasn't truly ready for.

And as a result, I've come to appreciate the slow progress in our relationship on a physical level. It's been different, but a good kind of different. It has forced me to focus more on him as a person, and sappy as it sounds, it's been wonderful.

We've talked and gotten to know each other, and we've taken the time to go through all these little steps, these markers I've always rushed through or skipped.

Tonight, we're crossing off another marker. It'll be the first time Joey will spend the night with me. In my bed. And

I'm more excited about that than I've ever been about fucking any of the pretty boys who have thrown themselves at my feet, which tells you how much I care about my boy.

"I'm strangely nervous," Joey says with a shy chuckle as he follows me into my bedroom, where I drop his weekend bag on the bed. "Like, I have all these tickles in my stomach. I used to feel like this when I had an important exam at school." He laughs again. "It's stupid, right?"

I click my tongue and shake my head at him. "Sweet boy, you know how I feel about you calling yourself stupid. It's a step for you, a big step, and it's okay to feel nervous."

"I want this," he says quickly, as if to assure me he hasn't changed his mind.

I smile at him as I take his clothes from the bag and place them on an empty shelf in my closet. "I know you do. Stop worrying about it. Daddy's got you."

The relief on his face is immediate, reminding me how important words are to my boy. He needs that reassurance, the praise, the reminders that he can let go. He loves it when I take charge, but he still needs to be reminded that it's okay to surrender.

I've planned a quiet night for us: watching a movie while eating on the couch. It's a simple meal, a creamy risotto with porcini I made before he came over, and if I do say so myself, it turned out nice. Halfway through the movie, Joey's eyes get heavy, and frequent blinking indicates he's losing the battle with his tiredness.

I stop the video and turn off the TV. "Time for bed," I say, my voice leaving no room for debate.

But Joey merely looks at me with gratitude. "Yes, Daddy. I'm tired."

I turn off all the lights, then lead him by the hand to my bedroom. "Raise your arms," I tell him, and without a second's hesitation, he obeys. I pull his shirt over his head, smiling at the happy expression on his face. His jeans are next, leaving him in his underwear.

"Go brush your teeth."

He cocks his head as he looks at me. "Is that okay? You telling me things like that?"

I frowned. "Why wouldn't it be?"

He shrugs, but there's a serious look on his face. "I don't know, but maybe because it crosses into another kind of Daddy kink?"

Ah, I get it now. Apparently, he's done some research, which I only applaud. The more you know, the better informed you are, the better you are able to make informed decisions. "You're talking about age play."

He nods. "We never talked about this, but is that something you would be interested in?"

I smile at him. "You're asking the wrong question, boy. It's not a matter of whether *I* would be interested in it, but if it's something that *you* would want to try."

He hesitates, then slowly shakes his head. "No. I've thought about it, and I read some blogs that explained what it looks like. I can see the appeal, but I don't think it's for me. I like you taking care of me, and I love knowing that I don't have anything to worry about, but I don't see myself dropping into a headspace where I'd be comfortable playing with toys or wearing a diaper. No offense to anyone who's into that because like I said, I can totally see the appeal, but not for me."

I pull him in and wrap my arms around him tightly. "I'm proud of you. I'm proud of you for doing your research and taking it seriously. But I'm even more proud of you for bringing it up, for communicating with me that that is not something you're interested in."

"Do you like it?"

His voice sounds muffled with his face hidden against my shoulder.

"I've experimented with it, and I don't mind some of it. Diaper play is definitely not my thing, and I wouldn't be the right Daddy for a boy who needs to be in his little headspace for longer periods. But if it had been something you'd want to try, I'd be up for that."

He sighs, and the last tension leaves his body. "Thank you, Daddy, for taking such good care of me."

I kiss the top of his head. "You're welcome, my sweet boy, though it's not something you need to thank me for. It's my privilege and my joy. I can't wait to spend the night with you and wake up together."

I make my night routine as short as possible, and we are in bed within minutes. Joey turns onto his side, then nestles himself against me, his arm wrapped around my stomach. In no time at all, he's asleep. It is so wonderfully normal and yet so special that I lie awake for a long time, reveling in the sensation of having my boy in my arms, of watching him sleep in the pale moonlight, which spills in through the curtains I haven't closed properly, of hearing him breathe. It may be normal and mundane, but it's special to me.

And as I lie awake, I plan a morning routine for us. After all, I have to do something to commemorate our first night together. And knowing how much he loved getting spanked, it's not hard to come up with something. I fall asleep with a smile on my face.

JOEY

. . .

Waking up with Daddy's strong arms around me is better than any heaven I've ever imagined. His skin is so warm against mine, his cock hard and pressed to the curve of my ass, his hot breath puffing against the back of my neck. I wiggle, testing the feeling of his erection. I'm not *quite* ready for that step, but the way my body heats at the feeling of it so close to such a sensitive area...yeah, I'm going to want that eventually.

Daddy groans sleepily, tightening his arms around me. "It's early. Go back to sleep."

I huff in annoyance but close my eyes again and lie still. I don't fall back asleep, but I'm more than happy to stay wrapped up in Daddy's arms for a few more hours, letting my mind find a peaceful place.

I can tell the moment Daddy really wakes up because he makes a happy sound in the back of his throat and thrusts his cock against me a few times before rolling away.

"Hey, where are you going?" I complain, flipping over so I can get close again. I put my head on his shoulder and curl against his large body.

"Not going anywhere, sweet boy, just needed to get ahold of myself for a second."

Feeling naughty and a little bit bold, I slip my hand under the blankets and past the waistband of his underwear, wrapping my fingers around the base of his cock. "What if I get ahold of you instead?" I tease, giving him a slow stroke.

His laugh turns into a groan, and he puts a hand over mine to stop my strokes. "I have other plans for you this morning."

"You do?" I ask. My cock thickens, pressing against his thigh.

"I do," he says. "You're going to stay beautifully naked for me and come with me to the kitchen so I can enjoy the view while I make you breakfast. Then I'm going to give you another spanking and a bath."

I moan, thrusting my erection against his leg. "Thank you, Daddy."

"Anything for my boy. After the bath, we're going to relax today, and then I have a special date planned for tonight."

I nuzzle my face into the crook of his neck and smile as I press my lips to his throat. "You're so good to me, Daddy."

He responds by kissing my forehead, dropping his hand to my ass and giving it a squeeze. "First things first, it's breakfast time."

I let him shuffle me out of bed. He pulls on a soft-looking bathrobe, his hungry eyes roaming over my naked body as I stand waiting for him. I may be an average forty-year-old man, but he makes me feel like the hottest person on the planet. My cock twitches under his gaze, and he grins.

The first thing Daddy does when we step out of the bedroom is check the thermostat. "Don't want you to get cold," he explains, turning it up a few degrees. It's not exactly cold in here, but my distinct lack of clothing certainly comes with a bit of a chill.

I follow him to the kitchen, and he takes one of the chairs from the table, turning it around so I'll be facing him while he cooks. "I want my boy on display for me, legs spread and arms behind your back."

"Yes, Daddy," I do as he says. With anyone else, the urge to cross my legs or my arms to hide parts of myself would be overwhelming, but being fully on display for Daddy makes me harder than ever, my cock standing up between my legs.

He sets to work, making what appears to be veggie omelets, giving me frequent heated looks and stopping every few minutes to walk over to me and tug at one of my nipples or stroke my cock or kiss me roughly.

"I wonder how you'd like it if I tied you up just like this and kept you here all day, making you come over and over," he muses, running his fingers through my hair and yanking my head forward to meet his lips for another hard kiss. I whimper into his mouth, the erotic image sending shockwaves through my body.

"Anything you want, Daddy," I gasp when he lets me go.

"Such a perfect boy," he praises, pressing a more gentle kiss to my lips before returning to the stove.

A few minutes later, he brings two plates over to the table, and I stand up so he can turn my chair around. I'm so turned on I can't believe he expects me to eat like this, but he gives me a stern look and points at my plate, so I force myself to take a bite. I moan around a mouthful of fluffy eggs and vegetables.

"This is so good, thank you, Daddy."

"You're welcome."

I manage to eat most of my breakfast, mainly because every time I slow down, he gives me that same commanding look. But all I can think about the whole time is the spanking he promised after.

I'm vibrating with excitement as he cleans up our dishes, and when he finally leads me to the living room and puts me over his knee just like he did the first night, I'm pretty sure I could die happily in that moment with his hand reddening my ass until I come all over his lap. And the bath we take afterward is even better than the orgasm itself. Daddy holds me and scrubs me clean, kissing me all over until we're both pruney and the water starts to get cold.

It turns out to be the perfect lazy day, and when evening

rolls around, I'm reluctant to let Daddy drag me off the couch for the date he has planned.

"But I'm comfy, Daddy," I whine, and he chuckles.

"Don't make me throw you over my shoulder and dress you myself," he warns, and I laugh.

"I'm not tiny like Pixie. I don't think you could carry me anywhere."

Daddy quirks an eyebrow at me. "Don't test me, boy."

I'm still chuckling at the thought as I roll off the couch and go to get dressed like he asked. He laid out clothes for me on the bed, and just like always, being taken care of feels like a warm blanket being wrapped around me. I smile while I get dressed, wondering where Daddy's taking me tonight and if it's possible he's falling in love with me like I'm falling in love with him.

Daddy helps me into the car, as always, and then tells me to close my eyes. He's gone for a few minutes, and then I hear the sound of the trunk opening and closing, and he gets into the car.

"You can open your eyes now," he says.

"This date is all very mysterious," I joke, and he grins.

As we head out of the city, I'm curious where we're going, but I don't bother to ask. Wherever Daddy decides to take me, I'm sure I'll like it.

He puts on his eighties playlist, and we both sing along to all our favorite hair metal bands, laughing at how badly we both sound but not letting that stop us. Eventually, he pulls off the road into what seems like the middle of nowhere. We're an hour outside of the city, and the last sign I saw said it's another sixty miles until the next town.

"You realize we're in the middle of the desert, right?" I ask.

"Yup, it's exactly the right spot to have a picnic and look at the stars."

"You remembered?"

"Of course I did."

We get out of the car, and he goes around to the trunk to pull out a large blanket and a picnic basket. "Did you have this lying around, or did you buy it especially for this date?" I ask with amusement, looking at the green wicker basket in the moonlight.

"What do you think?" he teases.

I brush a kiss to his cheek and smile. "Thank you, Daddy."

We spread out the blanket and get comfortable, the headlights from the car the only light for miles as we lie back and look up at the vast expanse of the night sky.

"This is amazing." I sigh happily, wiggling close to Daddy so I can put my head on his shoulder while we enjoy the view.

"It is. I can't believe I've gone so long without stopping to enjoy something like this."

"Me too. Sometimes you don't even realize what you were missing until it's right in front of you," I say.

He presses a kiss to the top of my head and tightens his arm around me. "Too true."

24

DADDY

I wake up with Joey plastered against me, gently snoring. It's a sure sign of how mushy my heart has gotten about him that I find his snores adorable. His arm is wrapped around my stomach, and he's holding on to me, even in his sleep. And even though I have to piss something awful, I'm content to lie here and wait for him to wake up, as I have been for the last few weeks when he's spent the night here.

I'm still amazed at how successful Kinky Boys' first video with Bear and Pixie has become. Viral doesn't even come close to describing it. Everyone and their mother is recommending it on social media, and I've seen the first short clips pop up on Pornhub. As long as they don't post the whole thing, it'll only lead to more viewers, so fine by me.

It's the best start of my studio I could've possibly dreamed of, and if the rest of the videos are even half as successful, Kinky Boys is off to a great start. The next video will go live today, and it's the one we did with Nick and Benny. The final version of that looked as amazing as I had expected it to be.

But no matter how happy and gratified I am with the success of Kinky Boys, it doesn't even come close to the joy in my soul over Joey. He just makes me so happy. It's never been like this for me. Sure, I've always loved being a Daddy, and I get great satisfaction out of taking care of my boys. But I've never felt the way I do with Joey.

I've never fallen for a man I thought was straight. I've never fallen for someone this quickly. And I sure as hell have never fallen for someone so deeply and completely as I have for Joey. Because what I feel for him has moved far beyond a mere infatuation, a crush, or really liking someone. This is love. This is the real thing, the kind of love that at some point will involve rings and promises and till death do us part.

And even better, I see that love reflected in Joey's eyes. We haven't talked about it yet, but I know we are on the same page. I'm not imagining things. We are falling in love with each other. Or better yet, we already *are* in love with each other. It's only a matter of time before we're ready to admit it, and I can't wait.

I want to wake up every morning with him in my arms. I want to make love to him, spank his gorgeous butt red, bring him pleasure, and watch him fall apart on my dick. I want to take care of him every single day, make sure he gets enough sleep, eats healthy, gets the rest and the exercise he needs. I want to grow old with him. And for the first time, that prospect doesn't scare me but exhilarates me.

As I watch him, still asleep in my arms, my heart fills with hope. My future is looking good, and who would've thought that a year ago? Everything has changed, and a lot of it is thanks to this wonderful man.

The doorbell snaps me out of my sappy thoughts, and with a frown, I check the clock. Who the hell would ring my doorbell at nine on a Saturday morning? Granted, we're sleeping in a little because we were up till late yesterday, but nine is not a normal time to disturb people on the weekend.

Just when I've decided to ignore it, whoever is at the door rings the bell again, longer this time. Worry blooms in my stomach. Has something happened? To one of my boys? To Joey's parents perhaps? I carefully disentangle myself from Joey and slide out of bed, covering him up again once I'm out. He makes a soft noise of displeasure, then resumes snoring.

I throw on a bathrobe and hurry to the door, where whoever the fuck it is is pressing the doorbell once again. I can't believe Joey is still asleep after this racket. He must have been really tired.

I open the door to find a young guy standing there, holding an envelope. Before I have the chance to inquire what he wants, he asks me, "Hunter Tronco?"

My stomach drops. "Yes," I say, knowing that denying it is useless anyway.

He hands me the papers. "You've been served." He tips his imaginary hat. "Have a nice day."

I stand in the open door long after he's gone, my heart racing and my stomach swirling so much I am scared of actually throwing up. Finally, I come to my senses and close the door. When I turn around, Joey stumbles out of the bedroom, looking all sleepy and crumpled.

"Hi, Daddy," he mumbles, stepping straight into my arms. I pull him close, dropping the papers on the floor.

"My sweet boy," I say, my voice choking up.

Just when I thought I had it all. Just when I thought the future was looking good. Hell, only minutes ago I was in bed, dreaming of a future with Joey, and now this. Even without reading the papers, I know what they will say.

Joey rubs his cheek against my bathrobe. "Who was that at the door? That's ridiculously early for a Saturday morning."

For one fleeting second, I debate lying to him. I don't want to burden him with this. I don't want him to look at me differently because my past is catching up with me. I don't want him to stop seeing me the way he does, with eyes full of love and trust, and I'm scared that if I open these papers, that will inevitably happen.

But I can't. I can't lie to him, because that would deny how much we mean to each other. He deserves more than that, and so I take a deep breath.

"I've been served papers."

Joey lets go of me immediately, stepping back, his face showing shock. "You've been served? Like, legal papers? For what?"

I slowly bend over and pick the papers up from the floor. "I haven't looked at them yet, but my guess is that Lex's parents are coming after me. I can't think of anything else it could be."

The shock on Joey's face transforms into devastation. "Oh no," he says softly. He hesitates for a second, then steps into my arms again, and I am grateful for his presence. "Let's open them together. You're not alone this time, Daddy."

Although I'm seconds away from crying, I can't hold back the words that once again well up in my heart. "I love you. I want you to know that. No matter what happens, no matter what these papers say or what the result of all this will be, I need you to know that I love you. I love you so much."

Joey lifts up his face, and this time, he takes the initiative to press a sweet, soft kiss on my lips that make my tears spill over. "I love you too. You know that. We may not have said the words, but we're not teenagers anymore. This is the real thing, you and me. And no matter what those papers say, we'll figure it out, and we'll get through this. Together."

I hold on to him like a lifeline. How is it possible to be this happy and this scared at the same time? Maybe I shouldn't be surprised. Love is like that, this anxiety-inducing combination of the warm and fuzzies, a joy unlike anything I've ever felt before, and at the same time, fear. Worries. A whole new level of stress. Maybe without those, it wouldn't be love.

Minutes later, with Joey on my lap, I finally open the envelope. I was right. Lex's parents may not have been able to convince the DA in New York to press charges against me, but that was not the only legal option available to them. This time, they're coming after me personally.

They've filed a civil wrongful death lawsuit against me in the state of Nevada. And while I know enough of the law to realize this can't lead to a prison sentence, I'm painfully aware that I could lose everything I own. If I lose this lawsuit, I could end up completely broke.

"Together," Joey reminds me, and I smile at him, ignoring the fear inside me.

"Together."

JOEY

DADDY LOVES ME. I know that's not the biggest takeaway from this otherwise crappy morning, but I can't help feeling a little bubbly inside anyway. Sitting in Daddy's lap with his arms around me, I know everything will be okay. It has to be.

Neither of us says anything for a while, and I swear I can hear the gears turning in Daddy's head the whole time.

"Today is the day when you normally visit your mom and bring your dad groceries, right?" he asks unexpectedly.

"Um, yeah."

"I'll come with you."

"What? You don't have to. You have a lot on your mind right now," I assure him. "In fact, I should probably get out of your hair and let you have space to think."

His arms tighten around me instantly. "No, I don't want space." He presses his face into the crook of my neck and breathes in deeply as if the scent of me alone is enough to calm whatever is raging inside him. "I want to go with you. I want to think about something else, and helping my boy with what he needs to do is just the thing."

"Okay, if you're sure?" I bite my bottom lip. Things have been better with my dad since I came out to him, but they're still a little tense.

"I'm sure," he says firmly, patting my leg to indicate I should get off his lap. "First, I want to take a shower with you. Then we'll go see your parents." He uses that tone that leaves no room for argument, and the sense of peace I've come to crave washes over me.

"Yes, Daddy," I say easily, getting to my feet and following him down the hall to the bathroom.

I only bothered to throw on one of Daddy's shirts before venturing out of the bedroom to see what the racket was about, and while the shower warms up, he slips it over my head, then kisses me. I sink into the feeling of his tongue thrusting into my mouth, sighing against his lips as he tangles his fingers through my hair to hold me in place as if I'd ever want to go anywhere while he's kissing me.

When we part, the small room is heavy with humidity, and the mirror is fogged up. Daddy slides off his robe and hangs it on the back of the door, then reaches into the top drawer of the bathroom sink. He pulls out a small bottle that can only be one thing, and I shiver with anticipation. We haven't had *sex* sex yet, and I haven't asked because I trust Daddy to decide when the time is right. If he thinks the time is right this morning, I'm completely on board with that. However, we both did go to the clinic and get tested last week.

He doesn't say anything about the lube, simply sets it on the edge of the tub and then pulls back the shower curtain and waves me inside. As soon as the curtain falls closed behind us, it feels like we're in our own little bubble world. There's nothing here but wet skin and the familiar scent of Daddy's soap filling the air. Here nothing can touch us, especially not bullshit lawsuits.

"Turn around for me, baby," Daddy says, filling his hands with soap and rubbing them together to work up a lather. I do as he says, letting out a contented sigh when he starts to run his sudsy hands over my shoulders and down my back, over the curve of my ass, dipping his fingers between my ass cheeks and teasing my hole. I gasp at the unexpected sensation, my cock hardening at the intensely intimate touch.

He plays with my entrance, circling and caressing it. I whimper desperately, pushing my ass back toward him.

"Please, Daddy."

"Not today, sweet boy," he says, his words at odds with his actions as he pushes the tip of his finger inside me, drawing another embarrassingly needy sound from me.

"But you grabbed lube." I barely manage to get out the short sentence while his finger thrust deeper, working me open with a gentle sting and the kind of fullness that's not enough and too much all at once.

"You're going to top me," he explains, not giving me time to register the words before his finger strokes something deep inside me that makes my cock jerk and my balls tighten so fast I'm surprised I don't come instantly.

"Oh my god," I moan, putting my hands on the shower wall to stay upright. "Daddy, please, please," I pant, thrusting helplessly, shaking from head to toe as he caresses the spot again.

"Greedy boy," he chides, his voice a deep growl as he presses his whole body against me from behind, pushing me harder against the wall as his finger continues to thrust inside me.

"Yes," I groan, my gut clenching and my cock throbbing. I *am* being a greedy boy, but it's so hard not to be when Daddy's teasing like this.

He chuckles at my answer, the sound rich and warm, settling in my chest and pushing me closer to the edge.

Then his fingers are gone. I cry out in frustration, and Daddy kisses the back of my neck and then gives me a hard slap on the ass, the sound twice as loud with the echo from the shower and the sting so good a pulse of precum drips from my cock.

"Grab the lube," he says, and I give a weak nod.

My hands tremble as I pick up the bottle he set on the side of the tub, and I hold it out to him. I know there's some prep that should happen, but I've never actually seen that part because the guys always prepped ahead of time for their scenes.

"I don't know what to do. Will you tell me what to do?"

He laughs again, and the way the grin twists on his lips, it hits me all over again that somehow this man loves me.

"Will I tell you what to do?" he repeats. "I think that's something you can count on, sweet boy."

I laugh along with him. I guess he's right. Him telling me what to do is a given. "I love you, Daddy," I say again, just because I can.

"I love you too, boy." He presses a kiss to my lips, and the jolt of it is almost as good as whatever he was doing inside me that nearly drove me insane. "Squeeze some lube into your hand and get yourself nice and slick," he instructs, and I do as he says.

I let out a quiet moan as I stroke my cock, admittedly spending more time spreading the lube than strictly necessary.

"Now, come here," Daddy says, turning around to face the wall, the same position I was in only a minute before. "Ease in nice and slow, okay?"

"Don't I need to, um, do anything else first?" I ask.

"I don't want any prep. I just want to feel my boy inside me." He looks at me over his shoulder, holding me with his intense gaze for several seconds. "Better hurry up before the water goes cold."

I step closer, holding the base of my cock steady in one hand and using the other to spread his ass cheeks apart. Every inch of my body feels like it's electrified as I press the tip of my erection to his puckered entrance. He's so tight it feels almost impossible to push inside him, but then the pressure gives way, and the heat of his body surrounds the head of my cock.

We both groan, and my eyelids flutter closed. It feels so good, *too* good.

"Daddy, I can't," I gasp, my balls tightening again along with the pit of my stomach, my cock throbbing, and I'm less than an inch inside him.

"You can," he argues. "You're such a good boy. You can give Daddy your cock."

A sob falls from my lips, and my hands find his hips while I press my face against the back of his shoulder. I push in a little further, his inner muscles squeezing around me. Inch by inch, I fill him, and rumbling sounds of pleasure from both of us echo through the bathroom.

I pull out and then thrust back in, over and over until the only thing that exists is the feeling of Daddy against me and all around me and the sound of our skin slapping. He meets my thrusts with his own, pushing back against me to teach me the rhythm he wants. Before long it feels more like he's fucking himself with my cock while I just hold on for the ride. My eyes roll back, and I dig my fingers into his waist.

"Harder," he grunts, and I piston my hips, rutting into him as hard as I can, my teeth clenched with the effort to hold back my orgasm. He tightens around me, and I whine helplessly. I can't hold on much longer. I can't. My rhythm stutters; my cock throbs. He clenches around me again, another deep sound reverberating from him, and my control snaps.

"Daddy," I moan, pleasure rushing over me as my cock spasms and pulses deep inside him, filling him up with my cum. He lets out a low growling sound, and his channel flutters around me with his orgasm.

I keep thrusting, chasing every last second of pleasure before my cock starts to soften and I'm forced to pull out. I slump against Daddy's back, rubbing my face against his wet skin, soaking him in.

"Oh, shit," I gasp, the water suddenly turning from hot to icy without any warning. Daddy chuckles, reaching over to shut the spray off.

"That's one way to hurry us along."

"Yeah, I would've preferred a few more minutes of shower cuddling," I grumble.

We step out of the shower, and Daddy grabs a towel off the shelf and takes his time drying me off while he stands there dripping. He's nearly dry by the time he runs the towel hastily over his own skin and then gives me a quick smack on the ass, telling me to get dressed so we can get the day moving.

I want to ask him how he's feeling about the lawsuit business, but I decide it's better if I give him some time to process, and if he wants to start by avoiding it, then that's what I'll let him do.

25

JOEY

Daddy is quiet as we drive over to my dad's place with a trunk full of groceries for him. I put my hand over his to offer silent support. He's been in his head a lot over the past week, wrestling with the lawsuit, I assume. And I've been doing my best to distract him whenever I can.

When we get there, we unload the groceries together, and miraculously, my dad turns off the TV and comes into the kitchen as we unpack them.

"How are you?" he asks somewhat awkwardly, but I'll take it. I shoot a quick smile at Daddy, and he grins back encouragingly.

"Good, Dad. What about you?"

"Good, good." He nods and reaches for one of the bags to help put things away.

We work in silence for a few minutes until Daddy catches my eye and gives me a pointed look, jerking his head toward my dad.

I take a deep breath and brace myself for a possible fight.

"Dad, we're going to swing by and see Mom after this if you want to come."

He stills with a bunch of bananas halfway to the fruit bowl. I chew on my lip, waiting for an answer, telling myself that even if he says no again or gets mad, things won't be any worse than they've already been.

"Okay," he answers in a clipped tone.

I let out a relieved breath. "Okay," I repeat.

I can't keep the grin off my face as we finish putting everything away, and then my dad puts on his shoes, and we all head out.

"We need to stop by the flower shop," my dad says as we pull out of the driveway. If there's anything sweeter than him wanting to bring my mom flowers, I can't think of what it would be.

"No problem, sir," Daddy agrees easily.

Armed with a bouquet of pink peonies, my mom's favorite, we head into the care facility.

"Hi, Joey," Julie greets in a perky voice, as usual. "Looks like you brought even more friends along this time."

"Yeah." I smile, reaching for the sign-in sheet. "This is my dad." I point the pen at him, and her smile widens, her eyes going a little gooey when she spots the flowers.

"Your wife is going to be so happy to see you. She talks about you all the time."

"She does?" His bottom lip trembles, and my heart breaks for him.

"Of course she talks about you, Dad," I say. He nods and clears his throat, clutching the flowers tighter. "Come on, let's go see her."

We all make our way down the hall to the main room, but when we get there, Daddy and I hang back a little to let my dad have a few minutes with her without us. He looks so nervous when he hands her the flowers, blushing and then rubbing the back of his neck with his free hand. He looks like he's a teenager asking someone on a date for the first time. My mom lights up, bringing the flowers to her nose to smell them and smiling at my dad with a smitten expression.

"I don't know if she remembers him right now or not, but I think she's falling in love with him all over again either way," I say with a smile.

"I think you're right." Daddy kisses my temple, draping his arm over my shoulders.

We end up spending a few hours sitting with her, watching some terrible soap opera on the TV while the two of them hold hands.

When it's time for us to leave, I almost hate to tear them apart again. My dad kisses her on the cheek and promises to visit again soon, and she says it was nice to meet him and that he reminds her of her husband. I've never seen someone look so devastated and loving all at once.

"It made her happy, even if she wasn't totally clear on what was happening the whole time," I assure him as we get into the car.

He sniffles and covertly wipes his eyes. "I think some part of her knew at least."

"I think so too," I agree. "I can bring you back next time I go if you want."

He nods and sniffles again, pulling a handkerchief out of his pocket.

When we get back to his place, I walk him inside while Daddy waits in the car.

"Dad, I really am sorry she couldn't live here with you anymore. It was the hardest decision I've ever had to make."

"It's for the best," he admits, putting a hand on my

shoulder and giving it a squeeze. For my father, that's the height of physical affection.

"Take care of yourself, and I'll see you in a few days."

My heart feels lighter as I climb back into the car. I never thought things would resolve with my dad, but knowing that he finally sees that the choice I made was necessary makes all the difference in the world.

"What now, Daddy?" I ask.

He takes a deep breath, then looks over at me. "I need to talk to my lawyer, but I think I might have to go to New York to see if I can take care of this without the court involved," Daddy says. I can tell he's been turning this over in his head all week, so all I do is nod. "It would help to have my boy with me. What do you say? Are you up for a trip to New York?"

"Would I, um, meet your family?" I ask, biting my bottom lip and tasting the coppery flavor of blood.

"Of course. I would've introduced you before now if they weren't on the other side of the country."

Thoughts of what they'll think of me and whether they'll feel like I'm good enough for their son flit through my mind, but I nod anyway. "I'd love to come with you. When are we leaving?"

"Let me talk to my lawyer, but most likely on the next flight out. Tonight if we can manage it."

"All right. If you drop me off at home, I'll pack a bag and be ready to go."

"Thank you. It helps, knowing you'll be by my side." He pulls me across the center console and into a kiss before starting the car and taking me home.

D*addy*

. . .

My lawyer in Vegas said it was a bad idea, but David, my New York-based lawyer I retained back when the DA was threatening with charges, agreed it was worth the try. It's not a good time for a trip now that we finally have Kinky Boys up and running, but it can't be helped.

The only thing that makes it bearable is Joey's presence. When I asked him to come with me, he didn't even hesitate. Of course, it helped that he already had permission from his boss. I guess that's one of the advantages of sleeping with your boss.

I would've preferred to take a flight during the day, but it turned out a red-eye was the quickest and most affordable option on such short notice. We leave Las Vegas shortly before midnight, so both of us mostly doze on the flight. Usually, I afford myself the luxury of booking business class, but no seats were available, so we're sitting shoulder to shoulder in economy. When it's Joey I'm pressed against, I find I don't mind so much.

When we land at Newark, both of us look a little disheveled, but we'll survive. I quickly check my phone, but David hasn't gotten back to me yet. He's been trying to set up the meeting I asked for, but apparently, he hasn't succeeded yet. That's okay because I have something else planned for us today.

"I thought you grew up in the city," Joey says as we sit in an Uber.

"I did. Born and raised in Brooklyn, but after my youngest sister had left for college, my parents moved to Jersey. There was no need for them to stay in the city anymore, since my dad changed jobs, so they wanted to move somewhere where they would get a little more bang for their buck. The city has become unaffordable for most families unless you're content living in a tiny little apartment you pay a couple of grand a month for."

"Kind of like LA," Joey says. "I'm glad I was able to buy a place when I started working for Ballsy Boys. I was able to sell it at a big profit when I moved to Vegas, giving me a nice little nest egg in case of harder times. If I would've had to buy it now, I would've never been able to."

"I think it's a problem in the big cities all across the country, and it's a damn shame. I love Brooklyn, and I loved growing up there, but I can totally understand why my parents left. Their place in Jersey has far less charm, but it's at least twice as big for half the money. You can't argue with that."

Along the way, we stop at Starbucks to grab some coffee and breakfast. I told my parents I would come by today, but I can hardly show up at their place at eight in the morning. So we take our time sipping our coffee, trying to push through our tiredness and lack of sleep. By the time we make it to my parents, it's just after nine.

"I'm nervous," Joey admits as we get out of the taxi.

I reach for his hand, then lift it to my mouth and press a soft kiss on it. "Sweet boy, don't you worry. They will love you."

"What if I accidentally call you Daddy? That would be awkward."

I shrug. "It's not like they don't know I'm up to my eyeballs in kink. If that's the most shocking thing they'll ever learn about me, I'll consider myself lucky. Truly, don't worry about it. I want you to be yourself, and they may not understand it, but I doubt they'll have a problem with it. Or at least, if they do, they won't show it."

Joey nods, biting his bottom lip, so I swipe my thumb

across it to dissuade him. "Stop torturing those lips. They are too beautiful to be abused like that."

"I'm sorry, Daddy. I'm really nervous."

Hmm, in my own worries over this trip, I may have forgotten about Joey's feelings. Meeting the parents is always stressful, but in his case even more. He's not the first man I'm bringing home to meet my parents, but we both know he's different than all the ones before. I see that as a good thing, and something tells me my parents will as well, but I can imagine Joey is worried it'll raise questions.

"I tell you what. As a thank-you and reward for coming with me, I'll spoil you tonight with a special surprise." Joey's eyes light up, and I smile. "That got your attention, didn't it?"

He nods. "What kind of surprise?" he asks, but then he rolls his eyes, I assume at himself. "Never mind. Forget I asked. Obviously, you're not going to tell me. Otherwise it wouldn't be a surprise."

I lean in for a quick kiss. "Trust me, you will love it."

The look he gives me makes my heart melts. "I know I will, Daddy."

Hand in hand, we make our way to the front door. Before I can even ring the bell, it swings wide open.

"Hunter," my mom says, and I let go of Joey's hand to accept her hug. "I'm so glad to see you. It's been too long."

I hold on to her a little longer than I normally would, and she tightens her embrace, maybe sensing that I need the feeling of safety she's always been able to give me as a kid. "It's good to see you, Mom."

We release each other, and I take Joey's hand again. "Mom, I want you to meet Joey, my boyfriend."

Her eyes widen for just a second before she catches herself. "Joey," she says, shaking his hand, "it's wonderful to meet you. Come on in."

Once inside, she closes the door behind us, and my dad steps into the hallway as well. His hug is brief but tight. "Son," he says, as always managing to pack a world of meaning in that one word. He's a man of few words, my dad, but he's always been a solid rock.

"Dad, this is Joey."

Joey and my dad shake hands, and my dad gives him a thorough look, then nods his approval. The tension in my body releases, and I smile as I follow my parents into the family room. My mom, bless her, offers us another round of coffee, which I gladly accept.

I didn't get my coffee snobbery from a stranger. My parents live a simple life for the most part, and they've never been prone to extravagant spending, but my father plunked down a lot of money for a really expensive coffee machine that makes the single best coffee I've ever had.

Joey lets out an involuntary moan when the flavor hits his tongue, and I chuckle. "Good, right?"

He nods. "Oh my God, this is the best coffee ever."

He doesn't know it, but complimenting his coffee is a sure-fire way to get my dad to like him.

"I'm glad you like it," my dad says, his voice ringing with pride.

"Like is too weak a word. This stuff is heavenly."

"I like you already," my dad jokes, and Joey blushes with that quick praise.

We chat for a little bit, my parents asking what Joey does for a living, then responding with respect when he shares he's working for me. Look, they know what I do. They knew I had a club in New York, and I told them what I was starting in Vegas. They may not understand it, but they're not critical or unsupportive. It's just a world that's so far outside their own experience that they have trouble connecting to it, and I get that.

"So what brings you to the city, Hunter?" my mom asks.

I let out a sigh. I've been open with my parents about what happened, not wanting them to get blindsided by hearing it from someone else. Besides, the press was pretty bad for a while, and they contacted my parents as well, trying to get quotes or salacious background stories on me.

"Lex's parents are suing me for wrongful death in a civil procedure," I say.

My mom gasps, then covers her mouth with her hand. "I thought that whole thing was behind you."

"So did I. Unfortunately, they are convinced that what happened to their son was not an accident, and they want to see justice."

"So you'll have to be here when it goes to trial?" my mom asks.

I shake my head. "No, they filed in Nevada because that's where I live. They can't sue me here, since New York has no legal jurisdiction over me anymore. I don't live here, and I no longer own property here."

My dad studies me for a few seconds. "You're here to try to dissuade them from going through with the case," he says slowly.

"Yes," I admit. "I know it's a long shot, but I have to try it. My lawyer in Nevada is confident we will win the case, but I don't even want to have to go through the trouble. Not for me, but also not for them."

"I can't even imagine how much they must be hurting," my mom says, her voice soft. "Just the thought of something happening to you or your siblings... It makes it hard to breathe, you know? As a mother, I feel her pain."

Before I can respond, my phone rings. When I see it's David, I quickly take the call.

"David, what's the word?"

"They have agreed to a meeting, but they want their lawyer present."

"That's only smart. Lex's father is a lawyer himself. He's not stupid. What time?"

"Noon, at my office."

"Perfect, I'll be there. Did you hear back from the PI?"

"Yes. He's sent me some stuff we can definitely use."

"Can you send it to me so I can have a look at it? I don't want to shock them or hurt them."

"Will do. I'll see you in a few, Hunter. I hope we can get this settled."

"Me too," I say and end the call. "God, I hope so."

26

JOEY

Being left alone with Daddy's parents is a little awkward, but likely less awkward than going to sit in on a meeting with Lex's parents.

"You ever build a birdhouse?" his dad asks, putting down his newspaper as soon as Daddy takes off.

"Um...no?"

"Come on." He gets up and waves at me to follow him. I can certainly understand why they left New York. There's no way they would've had a nice house like this or a backyard. He leads me over to a red-and-white shed, painted like a classic barn, and pulls open the doors, grinning proudly. I peek inside to see what looks like a small workshop filled with various scraps of wood and a few completed projects on one side, a workbench and tools on the other.

"This is my man cave," he explains. "After I retired, I needed something to occupy myself, or my wife would've ended up strangling me," he says with a chuckle. "So I started woodworking."

When he asked about a birdhouse, I was picturing something basic with the typical four walls, a flimsy roof, and a hole for a door. These are decidedly *not* that. These are like the Taj Mahal of birdhouses.

"Wow, are these bird mansions for billionaire birds?" I joke, bending down to look at one that's painted with little fake windows complete with shutters.

His dad chuckles. "I go a little overboard, but it's fun."

"I bet. I've never been all that handy, so these are impressive as hell."

"You should've seen my first few, all crooked and barely held together, but I got the hang of it eventually."

"That's really cool. Thanks for showing me these."

"My pleasure. I'm glad my son brought you home. His mother and I were worried about him after what happened. Truth be told, we were worried about him before that too."

"Because of the...um...the type of club he owned?" If there's a more uncomfortable conversation I could have with my boyfriend's dad, I'd like to know what it is.

"No, no. We may not understand all that, but it was obvious it made him happy, so that was good enough for us. We were worried about him finding someone to settle down with. We've only ever wanted him to be happy."

I nod in understanding. "He's a good man," I offer. "He takes good care of me, and I love him very much."

He beams. "I'm so glad to hear that. I know his mother is thrilled that you're here too. Be prepared because she's bound to cook an over-the-top dinner tonight to welcome you to the family."

My throat tightens, words failing me at such kind words. "That means a lot to me."

"So, how does a person get into the porn industry anyway?" he asks with amusement.

"Hard to say," I answer with a chuckle.

"Pun intended?" he jokes, and my face heats. Okay, sexual innuendos are *definitely* more uncomfortable.

"Oh my god, I can see where Hunter gets it."

He laughs. "We've always been a very open family. I guess it shouldn't have surprised us at all when Hunter wanted to work in such sex-heavy industries. It was never a taboo subject around here."

"I think that's nice. You get to know who he really is instead of him feeling like he needs to lie or hide things from you. I think more parents should be that way."

"Agreed. Do you get along with your parents?"

I smile, thinking back to my last interaction with my dad. "We've had some issues, but we're getting there," I assure him.

"Good, good. Family is important."

"Couldn't agree more."

"So, what do you say I show you how to build a birdhouse while we wait for Hunter to get home?"

"Sure, let's do it," I say gamely, rolling up my sleeves and preparing to make a fool of myself.

DADDY

SITTING in the big meeting room in David's firm, I feel like a man who's about to face a firing squad. I keep telling myself that I have nothing to lose, which is true. Worst-case scenario, the meeting ends with them walking out in anger, and we go to trial. Since that's the outcome now anyway, that's not worse than where we're at right now.

Best-case scenario, I show them how useless going to trial would be, and we reach a solution. A pipe dream?

Maybe. But I can't help but think it's worth trying. It's such a cliché to say what a deceased person would or would not have wanted, but in this case, it rings so true.

Lex loved our club. He loved the community. He loved being a boy so much that he was willing to risk his health and ultimately his life to be a part of it. He would've never wanted this, though that's not an argument I will ever utter in front of his parents. That would be disrespectful, considering I've met him only a few times, whereas he is their son.

I've never met his parents. I've seen pictures of them, watched an interview they did for a local channel, but we never met in person. But when they walk into the boardroom, they're older than how I remembered them. Tired. They greet me with a curt nod, no handshake for the man who killed their son. Fair enough.

Their lawyer, a sharply dressed guy named Michael Swan, could have been David's brother. David told me he knew him well, and that they had both worked together on various cases as well as been on opposite sides. He called him smart as a whip, aggressive, but fair. I guess that's the best I could have hoped for.

"Let me start by saying that my clients and I are not entirely sure what the purpose of this meeting is," Swan says.

David gestures at me. "I'll give the floor to my client. This was his initiative."

I take a deep breath, mentally rehearsing the speech I've prepared. I didn't want to write talking points down, scared that it would come across as too slick, too studied.

"Mr. and Mrs. Altman, thank you for agreeing to meet me here today. I can only imagine how hard this must be for you. I'm aware it sounds like a horrible cliché, but I would be amiss if I didn't start by saying how sorry I am for your son's death."

"Those are empty words," Mr. Altman snaps, and I nod.

"I understand, but I hope that by the end of this meeting, you'll have come to a different conclusion."

He mumbles something that sounds a lot like "I doubt it," but I let it go. "I didn't know Lex very well. I only met him a few times, and we weren't close to anything resembling friendship. We were acquaintances, and maybe not even that. All I knew about him was what he told me when he became a member at my club."

"You should've never let someone so young join a club like yours," Mr. Altman says, his voice ringing with bitterness.

"Respectfully, sir, I disagree. We have a legal age in this country for a reason, and my club's age limit is even higher. Twenty-one, that's when you can become a member. And we have all ID documents checked by one of our senior members who used to work for the FBI and can spot a fake document a mile away."

"If you hadn't let him join, he would've still been alive," Mr. Altman says.

Here we go. This is the part that will be hard for them to hear, but it's also the part that's necessary for them to understand. "As much as I'd love to leave you in that illusion, it's not true. Ours was not the first club Lex attended."

Mr. Altman pales slightly while his wife lets out a little gasp. "What are you talking about?" he asks.

"As a first preparation for the lawsuit, I've retained the services of a highly respectable private investigator to dig into Lex's background. Not to find dirt on him, because honestly, that would probably only work to my disadvantage. No, what I was hoping to find and what he did discover was that Lex's love for kink was not a recent thing."

"We would've known." It's the first time Mrs. Altman speaks up. "If he was into... That kind of thing, we would have known."

"Ma'am, when he was in college, an undergrad at Harvard law, he belonged to a club in Boston that lets people join when they are eighteen. He attended that club every chance he got."

After I drop that bombshell, the room becomes deathly quiet. His parents look at each other, shock painted all over their faces. "You're lying," Mr. Altman finally says, turning his attention back to me, but his voice doesn't pack the punch it did earlier.

"I understand this is not a world you are familiar with, not a world that you understand. But I do. I've owned my club for ten years, and before, I was active in the scene for another ten. This may be hard for both of you to hear, but this scene, this type of kink, it was what Lex craved. He sought it in Boston, where he played regularly in that club, doing the same kind of scenes he did in my club, and he sought it in my club as well. I have the names of several Doms he played with who are willing to talk to you."

"Threatening to paint him in a bad light won't work as a tactic to avoid a lawsuit," their lawyer says. "Any dirt you dig up on Lex will be paid back to you tenfold in the skeletons we'll uncover from your closet."

I lean forward on the table, folding my hands. "You don't understand. What that PI discovered about Lex, I don't consider dirt. It's the truth. It's who he was. I don't have kids myself, so I can't understand what a disappointment and shock it must be for you as parents to find out that your son had a life you knew nothing about, but those are the facts.

He wanted to be a *boy*, as we call it. He wanted to play with a Daddy. And nowhere, not in Boston, not in my club, not in any of the parties he attended that we have evidence of as well, did he ever disclose he had a medical condition."

His dad shakes his head vehemently. "That doesn't make sense. Lex was smart. He would've never risked his life like that."

"Sir, do you really believe that if he had disclosed his condition, I would've let him into the club? That I would've let him play? And not just me, but the club in Boston as well? The other parties he attended, all organized by respectable Doms in our community? None of us would've let him play. We would've all recognized the risks. He knew that. He knew that the only way he could play was by keeping his medical condition a secret."

A quiet sob echoes through the room, and Mrs. Altman covers her mouth with her hand, her eyes filling up with tears.

"How could he do that? I don't understand why he would risk his life just to..." Mr. Altman swallows. "Just to engage in something so *wrong* and depraved."

God, I have to tread so lightly here. He is a grieving father, someone who has never been exposed to the community, to kink in general. It's hard to make him understand that this lifestyle is more than a hobby, more than something we engage in for fun. It's who we are. It's what a lot, if not most, of us need to live a full and complete life.

"I've been a Daddy since I was in my twenties, just a few years older than Lex was. All my life, it's not just what I've done, but who I've been. Every relationship I've ever had was centered around it. And while I started out as an all-round Dom, I quickly gravitated toward scenes where I could express that part of my identity."

"It's unhealthy," Mr. Altman says, some of his previous fire back. "It's perverse and predatory, the way you prey on such young men."

Forgive me, sweet boy. Then I say, "Actually, Mr. Altman, my boyfriend is only two years younger than me. Being a Daddy isn't about age, though I'll admit that most of my boys have been much younger than me. It's about a dynamic. It's about wanting to take care of someone, making sure their every need is met, about keeping them safe."

"Well, then you certainly did a shitty job with Lex because if you'd been a good Daddy or whatever you call it to him, he would still be alive!"

After Mr. Altman's outburst, silence descends in the room, but I'm not offended by his words. It's the same thing I've been blaming myself for. I need to say what's in my heart, even knowing David is going to ream me out for this afterward, considering this could very well be used against me.

"I know, Mr. Altman. Trust me, I know. I've gone over every scene I did with him, over every minute of our conversation when he applied for membership. I keep playing those images in my mind, wondering where I dropped the ball, where I missed cues, misinterpreted information."

"Hunter," David says in a warning tone, but I hold up a finger.

"No, David, let me talk. I have enough belief in both our legal system and humanity that I think I can express my sense of guilt, my self-doubt, without admitting to being guilty. Those two things are different. Lex's death wasn't my fault. I know that rationally, but emotionally, it will take me a long time to forgive myself for what happened."

Mrs. Altman is crying openly now, quiet sobs that break my heart. I don't know what to tell her other than what I've said already. But is she hearing it? Does she understand what I'm trying to say?

"All I want is to prevent other parents from going through what we're dealing with," Mr. Altman says, suddenly sounding tired and defeated.

"With all due respect, Mr. Altman," David says. "But that's not true. You're a lawyer. You know how this works. If there had been negligence on Mr. Tronco's part, the DA would've pressed the lawsuit against him. They couldn't find fault. His procedures were watertight, and the only reason this happened is that your son omitted crucial information on his medical release. This lawsuit will never prevent other parents from experiencing this, because it's not aimed at the procedures in the club, at weaknesses or mistakes Mr. Tronco or any of his employees made. It's aimed at Mr. Tronco himself, at making him pay for what happened to your son. And as much as I sympathize with your loss, Mr. Tronco is not at fault for Lex's death."

I catch a subtle signal from Swan to David, so I'm not surprised when David rises and says, "We'll give you a few minutes to discuss this with each other."

27

JOEY

Daddy's gone for several hours, and by the time he gets back, his mom *does* have an elaborate dinner nearly ready to be served.

"How'd it go?" I ask, giving him a kiss when he pulls me into his arms.

Daddy sighs, and I can feel the weight of it through my whole body. I tense, waiting for him to give me terrible news. He knew going in that talking to Lex's parents might only make things worse, but even if he has to face a full lawsuit, I'll be right by his side the whole time.

My biggest fear is that he'll have to put Kinky Boys on hold or shut down the studio altogether before we've hardly even gotten it off the ground. This could ruin him financially, but I'm more worried about what it might do to him emotionally to be dragged through all the details all over again and that he'll find new reasons to blame himself for what happened.

"They dropped the lawsuit," he says.

"What?" I gasp. "Oh my god, you scared me. Did they really?"

"Sorry, I didn't mean to freak you out. I'm drained from the whole thing." He kisses the top of my head. "It was difficult having to talk with them and trying to show them the light about a huge part of their son's life that he'd hidden from them. I think in the end, Mr. Altman saw reason and managed to convince his wife that bringing up the past over and over wasn't going to bring their son back."

"I can't imagine how difficult this must've been for them," his mom says sympathetically.

"I know. It's why I wanted to talk to them face-to-face. I needed them to see I'm not a monster. I may not have known their son well, but I cared about him just like I cared about every sub I've ever played with. What happened was a tragedy."

"So, it's all over now?" I ask.

"It's all over now," Daddy assures me. "And I smell dinner, so why don't we eat."

"Everything smells delicious, Mrs. Tronco," I agree. "Do you need help with anything?"

"Aren't you sweet?" she coos. "Call me mom. And why don't you boys bring everything to the table for me."

"Okay," I say with a smile, feeling all warm and fuzzy inside at his parents' easy acceptance of me.

Hunter and I help bring the food over to the table, and when it's time to sit down, he pulls my chair out for me.

"Thank you, Daddy," I say, catching my words a few seconds too late, my cheeks flaming. I glance over at his parents seated across the table from us, but neither of them seems to think anything of it. I look back at Daddy in surprise, and he just lifts his eyebrows and gives me an I-told-you-so grin.

"So, Joey, what made you get into filmmaking?" his mom asks.

"I was kind of a dorky kid," I confess. "I didn't have many friends when I was young, so I spent a lot of time watching movies. I became really interested in not just the stories but also the artistry of the way certain shots were filmed, how a wide shot or a close shot could change the whole tone of a scene. By high school, I had a few friends, and we spent our weekends making god-awful movies. One of my buddies would write the scripts, and our other friends would be the actors, and I'd film them. It was silly, but when the movies were finished, we'd make our parents all gather around to watch. They always indulged us, acting like they were going to the premieres of major motion pictures." I grin at the memory. "It wasn't a surprise to anyone when I enrolled in film school after high school."

"And then you ended up filming porn?" his mom asks as casual as ever. I snort into my glass of water, my face flaming again.

Daddy pats me on the back to soothe my coughing fit, and I set my glass down. "Um, yeah. Life takes strange turns sometimes, I guess, but I'm proud of the work I do. I've made a good living and won awards for my cinematography, and it led me to Hunter, so I can't think of a better path I could've taken than that." I glance over at Daddy to find him smiling at me with so much warmth and affection in his eyes it nearly stops my heart.

"I can't think of a better path either," he says, leaning in and kissing me sweetly.

"I think I'm going to cry," his mom says, fanning her eyes. "I'm just so happy you finally have someone."

"Me too," Hunter agrees.

"Me three," I chime in.

"We'd better head out," Daddy says once dinner is finished and everything is cleaned up.

"Where are we going?" I ask.

"I booked us a hotel room for the night. I didn't think we'd both fit in the twin bed that's still in my old bedroom," he says and then dips his head so his lips are right beside my ear. "And I didn't think you'd want my parents to hear the spanking I'm planning to give you."

I shiver and lean into him. "You think of everything, Daddy."

"That's my job," he says with a grin, pulling me in for a quick kiss.

Daddy

"Here's the plan," I say as soon as we step into our hotel room, and I close the door firmly behind me, locking it. God, I'm relieved. It's like a heavy weight has been lifted off my chest, and I want nothing more than to celebrate with my boy. "Your reward has two parts. One part is my call, and the other part you get to choose. Sound fair?"

Joey looks at me with a heated expression, then licks his lips. "Yes, Daddy."

"I already told you what my reward is for you. I'm going to spank that gorgeous, strong ass of yours a beautiful shade of red. After that, the ball is in your court. The only requirement for whatever you choose as a reward is that it has to be something we can do right here, right now. Oh, and a second requirement is that we can do it naked. I have a powerful yearning to cuddle with you, so let's start with that."

"Are you having second thoughts about the spanking? Would you rather cuddle with me than spank me?" Joey teases while I walk toward the room's thermostat and crank it up.

I booked us a nice, luxurious room at an airport hotel near Newark, so we can easily catch a shuttle to the airport tomorrow morning. It'll be worth every penny.

I chuckle, unbuttoning my dress shirt with quick fingers. The sooner my boy and I are both naked, the better. "No, I'm not. As much as I love cuddling with you, I had something more... active in mind. But if you'd choose cuddling as a reward, I would absolutely not object."

Joey laughs. "I had something more...active in mind as well."

Within seconds, our clothes are off. After taking some supplies out of the bag I packed and putting them on a little coffee table, I lower myself into a chair that looks more comfortable than it is, the coarse fabric slightly itching my skin. It'll have to do. I gesture Joey over with one finger, and he hurries toward me eagerly.

There is no hesitation as he parks himself onto my lap, and I love it. I hold him close, letting my hands roam his body as if to reacquaint myself with every strong muscle, every soft spot, every bit of skin. He breathes out a hum of pleasure.

"You're beautiful," I tell him softly, kissing his neck with little licks and bites. I love how he responds to my every touch. He's always been eager for physical contact, and it hasn't diminished a bit over the last few weeks.

"Thank you, Daddy. So are you. I always get a tingling in my stomach every time I look at you," he admits, and my heart melts.

"You're such a sweet boy. Daddy loves you so much."

For a while, we just sit and cuddle, my body slowly awakening to Joey's presence, to his warm skin against mine, to the wonderful sensation of my fingertips exploring his back, his neck, his arms. I love how he shivers, how he makes these little sounds. Gasps. Moans. A whimper. So uninhibited. So honest and pure.

"What would you like from Daddy? What reward would you like, boy?"

Joey looks up at me with sweet eyes. "I want you to fuck me, Daddy. I'm ready."

I search his face, looking for any indication that he still has doubts but finding none. A rush travels through my body, putting all my nerves on high alert. I've been looking forward to this, and though I would've been perfectly fine waiting longer or never doing it at all, since Joey matters more to me than this act, now that we're here, I can't wait. I realize the magnitude of what he's proposing. He may not be a virgin, but he's offering me to be his first in something special.

"That's a big gift you're giving me, and I promise you I will cherish it. We'll go slow, okay?"

Joey nods. "But, Daddy, I still want the spanking."

"No worries, sweet boy. Daddy will make you fly."

With a little bit of pressure on his arms, Joey gets the hint and turns around to straddle me. I immediately take his mouth in a hot kiss, unable to wait any longer to taste him again. He sighs into my mouth, opening up and letting me in. I circle my arms around his waist, then let them travel lower, grabbing his ass with my hands as I ravage his mouth.

He really is beautiful, and I have a special fondness for his ass. I know Joey is insecure about his body at times, and I can relate to that because it's how I often feel as well. Neither of us is twenty anymore. But he shouldn't be. I can't get enough of his body, particularly his ass, and the thought of being inside him has me trembling with anticipation.

I take my time kissing him, kneading his ass and warming it up for my hands. It's always a double-edged sword because the more I stimulate his circulation, the more he will feel it. I don't want it to become too painful for him, so the challenge is to find that perfect balance where pain and pleasure are inextricable from each other.

Another gentle push and Joey gets off my lap, then drapes himself over my thighs. I swat his ass lightly. "Mmm, I've been looking forward to this all day."

"Me too, Daddy."

What a perfect answer from my perfect boy. I start slowly, letting my hands rain down with gentle slaps, spreading them out all over his buttocks and the back of his thighs. Joey leans into it, his body surrendering. Within a minute or two, his skin is glowing, and his wet cock is leaving traces on my leg.

"Since this is a reward, sweet boy, you can come at any time...and as often as you want."

Joey makes an appreciative noise, and I rub his flaming ass a bit before starting on the second round of slaps. I put a bit more force behind them, but I still spread them out, and a mix of excitement and satisfaction hums through my blood the way his skin reddens for me.

"Daddy..." Joey sighs, uttering the most beautiful word on the planet.

"I'm so proud to have you as my boyfriend, as my perfect boy. You're perfect for me. You make me so happy."

"Daddy," Joey says again, and it's halfway between a sob and a plea.

I keep swatting him with one hand, reaching for the lube with my other hand. It's a little tricky doing this with one hand, but I have years of experience and manage to squirt some onto my fingers. I don't know if he knows what I'm doing or if it's instinctual, but Joey spreads his legs, opening up that gorgeous hole for me. I tap it with a slick finger, and Joey pushes back, letting me in.

He takes that first finger with a soft grunt, and I sink it deep inside him, immediately curling it to hit that sensitive spot inside him. I don't have to question whether I found it because the low moan he lets out is all the proof I need. With a little experimenting, I set a rhythm where I alternate soft slaps with harder ones, finger-fucking him in between.

Joey squirms on my lap, and I let it go. I can't possibly expect him to stay still under these circumstances. Besides, I love the way he pushes against my fingers, against my hand in a silent invitation for more.

"So good, Daddy... So good," he babbles, and he has to be close, judging by how tightly strung his body is. He's fighting it, and I love him for it.

I debate stopping, not wanting him to come before I'm up to my balls inside my boy, but then I decide he has another round in him. This is a reward, so I can afford to be magnanimous.

I have three fingers in his ass now, and Joey takes them without a problem, a testament to how relaxed he is and how slow I've been working him open. "Are you ready for Daddy's cock, boy?" I ask, not even expecting a reply, but Joey surprises me.

"Please, yes. So much. Need you, Daddy. Don't want to come without you."

I pull out my fingers and give him a last swat on his ass, which is now red and radiating heat. "I can't wait to be inside you, my sweet boy. I promise you it will feel amazing."

I wish I could carry him to the bed, but that's a little

risky because I don't want to throw out my back. And no way in hell is my first time inside my boy going to be in this uncomfortable chair. Not when we have a soft and fluffy mattress available.

I help Joey stand up, holding on to him for a bit until he's steady, then pull him by the hand toward the bed.

"On your back, boy," I say. "I want to see your beautiful face when we do this."

Joey nods and climbs onto the bed, putting a pillow under his ass without me having to tell him. I guess he picked up a thing or two at work over the years.

I lower myself between his legs, taking a few seconds more to admire how stunning his ass is when it's all red and well spanked. This is definitely something we need to make a habit of. Luckily, we'll have a lifetime to do this. And where that thought would've scared the shit out of me merely months ago, it's now making me happier than I ever thought possible.

"Are you ready for me?" I check one last time, and Joey nods.

"More than ready, Daddy. I want this. I want you."

I line up my cock, then press against him, sinking inside him with ease. I go slow, inch by inch, watching Joey's face for any signal it's too much, too fast. But Joey holds my gaze, soft moans falling from his lips as his eyes darken with pleasure.

"Good?" I ask as I'm buried to the hilt inside him.

"Better than I ever imagined."

I start by thrusting slowly, but Joey wraps his arms around me, cants his hips, and encourages me to go faster with every move of his body. He's no fragile twink, no breakable boy, and I allow myself to release the tight hold on my self-control.

The next surge inside him is hard, and our combined grunts create intoxicating music. After that, it's a blur of hard thrusts, of Joey encouraging me with his body, with words that barely register with me, of a pleasure that builds and builds until it becomes so big inside me I can't hold back anymore.

"Daddy!" Joey cries out, and his body shakes and jerks underneath mine as he shoots his hot release between us. I made him come. I made my sweet boy come without ever touching him, without him ever touching himself, and the rush of that sends me over the edge.

My last thrusts are jerky, barely coordinated, fueled by a primal need to claim him, to fill him. And then I do, releasing deep inside him and staying there until my cock stops twitching.

With my last bit of energy, I wrap my arms around him and roll us onto our sides, preventing me from dropping on top of him with my full weight.

"Don't leave me yet, Daddy," Joey begs as my cock slips half out of him, and I smile.

"Lift up your leg," I tell him, and when he does, I push back in. It won't last long, not when my cock completely deflates, but I'm perfectly happy to stay inside him as long as I can.

"That better?" I ask him, and Joey nods, his eyes closed as he blindly seeks my mouth for a kiss.

We stay like this for a long time, Joey protesting every time I let go of him until I get the hint and embrace him tightly, touching him wherever I can. We'll regret falling asleep like this in the morning, but for now, it's paradise.

28

JOEY

The flight is entirely too early, especially considering how late Daddy and I stayed up touching and making love with each other until we finally passed out. It felt like the perfect way to celebrate Daddy being able to finally close such a painful chapter in his life.

I'm not sure what I expected bottoming to be like, but it was so much better than I ever could have guessed. It was fun to top Daddy in the shower last week, but giving up all my control to him last night and letting him have my body completely...it was beautiful, and it felt *so* right.

"Can we get coffee?" I ask as Daddy hustles me through the airport in search of our boarding gate.

He checks his watch. "Sure, we have enough time to grab some coffee before boarding starts."

"And donuts?" I ask hopefully. "Or oh, there's a Cinnabon. Please, Daddy?" I beg, my mouth watering at the sugary smell of cinnamon and frosting.

He sighs and shakes his head. "You can have a cinnamon roll now, but that's your last treat for the next two days."

"Daddy," I pout.

"There's enough sugar in those damn things to put a person into a diabetic coma."

"Fine," I groan. "One cinnamon roll and then nothing else for the rest of the day."

"*Two* days."

Drat, busted.

"Fiiiine," I grumble, but I don't miss the grin on Daddy's face. He likes that I'm getting comfortable enough as his boy to be a little bratty. I think I like it too. Not so bratty I'll miss out on a spanking but just bratty enough to keep him on his toes.

"There's our gate." He points just a little ways down from where the Cinnabon is. "Why don't you have a seat and I'll get you your breakfast."

"Thank you, Daddy." I kiss his cheek and head toward the gate he pointed to.

He finds me a few minutes later, handing me a cup of coffee and a cinnamon roll. He watches with barely concealed horror as I chow down on the gooey treat.

"You want a bite?" I offer him my fork with a frosting-covered bite.

"I'm going to have to pass on that one."

"Your loss," I tease, shoving the food into my mouth and letting out an exaggerated moan. Daddy quirks an eyebrow at me, and I can see the dirty thoughts written all over his face. I chuckle and take another bite.

By the time boarding starts, my cinnamon roll has been demolished and my coffee is gone. We find our seats, and our late night crashes over me again. I lean over and put my head on Daddy's shoulder, giving a big yawn.

"Sleep. I'll wake you when we land." He kisses the top of

my head, and a smile spreads over my lips as I let my eyes drift closed.

I sleep through the whole flight, groggily blinking and grumbling when Daddy gently shakes my shoulder to wake me up.

"We're home, sweetheart," he murmurs.

I sit up and groan at the crick in my neck. "I'm too old to sleep like that," I complain.

"I'll give you a neck massage a little later," he promises.

We packed light, so neither of us has any checked bags. I follow Daddy through the airport and to the parking lot where we paid to leave his car while we were gone.

"I don't want to go home," I pout as Daddy buckles me in. I know I should at least stop by my apartment to change my clothes and probably clean out my refrigerator because I honestly can't even remember the last time I was home long enough to eat there.

He chuckles and then goes around to the driver's side. "I don't want you to go home either. I like having you with me."

My stomach flutters happily. I wonder if the excitement of being wanted by Daddy and wanting him back will ever wear off. Something tells me it won't.

"What if...um...I could keep some clothes at your place maybe?" I suggest cautiously, not sure if this is an area I'm supposed to wait for Daddy to decide on. It's not like I'm talking about moving in together, just leaving a change of clothes there.

"What if you kept more than clothes there?" he counters.

"What do you mean? Like my razor and my favorite soap or something?" I much prefer using Daddy's soap so I can smell like him all day, but I'll bring whatever he wants over to his place.

"Like everything."

"Everything?" I repeat, not sure I'm understanding. "What would be at my place, then?"

"Hopefully the belongings of the new tenant," he teases.

"What?" He's not asking what I think he's asking, is he? "What do you mean?" I bite back my smile just in case I'm jumping to the wrong conclusion.

"I'm asking you to move in with me, sweet boy. What do you say? We can get a bigger, nicer place when the lease is up."

"You want me to move in with you?" I ask, my voice bubbling with excitement, half sure I'm still asleep on the plane and this is just a fantastic dream.

"I want to go to sleep with you every night and wake up next to you every morning. I want you naked in our kitchen while I cook, and in my shower, and in my life *completely*."

A lump forms in my throat, and all I can do at first is nod. No one has ever said anything so romantic to me in my life. I know it's not a marriage proposal or anything like that, but it makes everything feel even more real. This isn't a game or something fun and shiny for a little while. He's talking about merging our lives to create something even better.

"Yes, Daddy," I answer in a near whisper because I'm still afraid my voice is going to crack with emotion. "I want to move in with you."

"Come here, boy," he growls, tugging me halfway across the center console to kiss me hungrily, tangling his fingers in my hair and licking into my mouth like I'm his last meal.

"I love you, Daddy."

"I love you too, boy, and I can't wait to see what we can build together."

. . .

The End

Coming Soon: Ziggy (Kinky Boys 2)

BOOKS BY NORA PHOENIX

🎧 means also available in audio book

Perfect Hands Series

Raw, emotional, both sweet and sexy, with a solid dash of kink, that's the Perfect Hands series. All books can be read as standalones.

- **Firm Hand** (daddy care with a younger daddy and an older boy) 🎧
- **Gentle Hand** (sweet daddy care with age play) 🎧
- **Naughty Hand** (a holiday novella to read after Firm Hand and Gentle Hand)

No Shame Series

If you love steamy MM romance with a little twist, you'll love the No Shame series. Sexy, emotional, with a bit of suspense and all the feels. Make sure to read in order, as this is a series with a continuing storyline.

- **No Filter** 🎧

- **No Limits** 🎧
- **No Fear** 🎧
- **No Shame** 🎧
- **No Angel** 🎧

And for all the fun, grab the **No Shame box set** 🎧 which includes all five books plus exclusive bonus chapters and deleted scenes.

Irresistible Omegas Series

An mpreg series with all the heat, epic world building, poly romances (the first two books are MMMM and the rest of the series is MMM), a bit of suspense, and characters that will stay with you for a long time. This is a continuing series, so read in order.

- **Alpha's Sacrifice**
- **Alpha's Submission**
- **Beta's Surrender**
- **Alpha's Pride**
- **Beta's Strength**
- **Omega's Protector**
- **Alpha's Obedience**
- **Omega's Power**

Ballsy Boys Series

Sexy porn stars looking for real love! Expect plenty of steam, but all the feels as well. They can be read as stand-alones, but are more fun when read in order.

- **Ballsy** (free prequel)
- **Rebel** 🎧
- **Tank** 🎧

- **Heart**
- **Campy**
- **Pixie**

Ignite Series

An epic dystopian sci-fi trilogy (one book out, two more to follow) where three men have to not only escape a government that wants to jail them for being gay but aliens as well. Slow burn MMM romance.

- **Ignite** 🎧
- **Smolder**

Stand Alones

I also have a few stand alones, so check these out!

- **Kissing the Teacher** (sexy daddy kink between a college prof and his student. Age gap, no ABDL) 🎧
- **The Time of My Life** (two men meet at a TV singing contest)
- **Shipping the Captain** (falling for the boss on a cruise ship)
- **Snow Way Out** (snowed in with an age gap, a size difference, and a bossy twink)

BOOKS BY K.M. NEUHOLD

Stand Alones
  Change of Heart

Love Logic
  Rocket Science

Heathens Ink
  Rescue Me
  Going Commando
  From Ashes
  Shattered Pieces
  Inked in Vegas
  Flash Me

Inked
  Unraveled
  Uncomplicated
  Unexpected

Replay

Face the Music
Play it by Ear
Beat of Their Own Drum
Strike a Chord

Working Out The Kinks
Stay
Heel

Ballsy Boys
Rebel
Tank
Heart
Campy
Pixie

Short and Sweet Stand Alones
That One Summer
Always You
Kiss and Run

MORE ABOUT NORA PHOENIX

Would you like the long or the short version of my bio? The short? You got it.

I write steamy gay romance books and I love it. I also love reading books. Books are everything.

How was that? A little more detail? Gotcha.

I started writing my first stories when I was a teen...on a freaking typewriter. I still have these, and they're adorably romantic. And bad, haha. Fear of failing kept me from following my dream to become a romance author, so you can imagine how proud and ecstatic I am that I finally overcame my fears and self doubt and did it. I adore my genre because I love writing and reading about flawed, strong men who are just a tad broken..but find their happy ever after anyway.

My favorite books to read are pretty much all MM/gay romances as long as it has a happy end. Kink is a plus... Aside from that, I also read a lot of nonfiction and not just books on writing. Popular psychology is a favorite topic of mine and so are self help and sociology.

Hobbies? Ain't nobody got time for that. Just kidding. I

love traveling, spending time near the ocean, and hiking. But I love books more.

Come hang out with me in my Facebook Group Nora's Nook where I share previews, sneak peeks, freebies, fun stuff, and much more:

https://www.facebook.com/groups/norasnook/

Wanna get first dibs on freebies, updates, sales, and more? Sign up for my newsletter (no spamming your inbox full... promise!) here:

http://www.noraphoenix.com/newsletter/

You can also stalk me on Twitter:
https://twitter.com/NoraPhoenixMM
On Instagram:
https://www.instagram.com/nora.phoenix/
On Bookbub:
https://www.bookbub.com/profile/nora-phoenix

MORE ABOUT K.M. NEUHOLD

Author K.M.Neuhold is a complete romance junkie, a total sap in every way. She started her journey as an author in new adult, MF romance, but after a chance reading of an MM book she was completely hooked on everything about lovely- and sometimes damaged- men finding their Happily Ever After together.

She has a strong passion for writing characters with a lot of heart and soul, and a bit of humor as well. And she fully admits that her OCD tendencies of making sure every side character has a full backstory will likely always lead to every book having a spin-off or series.

When she's not writing she's a lion tamer, an astronaut, and a superhero...just kidding, she's likely watching Netflix and snuggling with her husky while her amazing husband brings her coffee.

Stalk Me
Website: www.authorkmneuhold.com
Email: kmneuhold@gmail.com
Instagram: @KMNeuhold

Twitter: @KMNeuhold

Bookbub: https://goo.gl/MV6UXp

Join my mailing list for special bonus scenes and teasers: https://landing.mailerlite.com/webforms/landing/m4p6v2

Facebook Reader Group Neuhold's Nerds: You want to be here, we have crazy amounts of fun: http://facebook.com/groups/kmneuhold